"I'm not Clair—
I'm her cousin."

Corinne tried to ignore the anger in Juan's eyes. "Clair couldn't come," she said, "and rather than disappoint her grandfather—"

"Rather than lose out on her inheritance, you mean?" Juan queried harshly. "And what do you gain by being her accomplice?" he asked. "A share in the proceeds?"

"No, I...." She could have explained how Clair had blackmailed her, but she felt she had told Juan enough. He might have been the business partner of Clair's grandfather but what hold did he have over Corinne?

"You have no right to condemn me for helping my cousin," she said. "You're just as interested in the inheritance as Clair is."

"And that's not all I'm interested in, Miss Suter," he said, "as you may soon find out...."

JANE CORRIE
is also the author of these
Harlequin Romances

Many of these titles are available at your local bookseller.

For a free catalogue listing all available Harlequin Romances
and Harlequin Presents, send your name and address to:

HARLEQUIN READER SERVICE,
M.P.O. Box 707, Niagara Falls, NY 14302
Canadian address: Stratford, Ontario N5A 6W2

Island Fiesta

by

JANE CORRIE

Harlequin Books

TORONTO • LONDON • LOS ANGELES • AMSTERDAM
SYDNEY • HAMBURG • PARIS • STOCKHOLM • ATHENS • TOKYO

Original hardcover edition published in 1980
by Mills & Boon Limited

ISBN 0-373-02384-7

Harlequin edition published February 1981

CHAPTER ONE

Corinne Suter stared at her cousin. 'Go in your place?' she said in an incredulous voice. 'All that way? I couldn't! For goodness' sake, Clair, where did you get such a crazy idea from?' she demanded.

Clair Suter met Corinne's astounded stare with an impatient shake of her ash-blonde hair. 'Well, I can't go, can I?' she replied irritably, and waved an elegant hand towards her left foot encased in plaster of paris. 'Besides,' she added in a bored voice, 'deathbed scenes are definitely not my forte.'

Corinne's soft mouth set. 'I wouldn't have said that they were mine, either,' she said firmly. 'And he is your grandfather. Quite apart from the fact that he doesn't know me, what do you hope to gain from it?' she asked in exasperation.

'He doesn't know me either,' said Clair, and gave a casual shrug. 'It won't matter anyway. He won't look for any family likeness; he went blind about two years ago. All you do is say you're me, he'll only be waiting to hear an English voice, and he'll believe you.'

Corinne's dark blue eyes widened, and she gave Clair a look of distaste. 'Well, you'll have to find someone else, Clair. If all he needs is an English voice, you won't find it too hard finding someone to stand in for you, particularly as you're paying the fare out there. I imagine someone would jump at it.' She got up from her chair and walked restlessly to the window, then looked back at Clair. 'How you can even think of deceiving him is beyond me. I know your mother walked out of her home all those years ago, but he is still your grandfather. Why don't you write to him and tell him that you've broken your ankle and can't possibly pay him a visit? Someone will read the letter to him. That letter you received didn't actually say he was dying, did it?' she added pleadingly.

Clair's thoughtful light blue eyes rested on Corinne in an almost calculating way. 'No, it didn't,' she replied brusquely. 'But this Juan Martel, whoever he is, was most insistent that I should lose no time in going to see my grandfather,' she gave another casual shrug. 'I can't see any other reason for the urgency, can you?' she asked Corinne. 'And that's why it must be you,' she added adamantly. 'Apart from the fact that you know all there is to know about the family, where else could I find another Clair Suter?' she queried with an ironic smile.

Corinne looked away from her quickly. The bald fact that she had been christened Clair she could not deny, but as the respective mothers of the girls had perversely insisted on naming their daughters Clair, an old family name that went back several centuries and was a source of family pride, the fact had caused much friction between the families. In the end, Clair's mother had won the battle by the mere fact that she had given birth to her daughter precisely one hour before her sister-in-law had had Corinne, and although defeated Corinne's mother had still christened her daughter Clair, but for the sake of peace the child was known by her second name, Corinne. It would have been so much simpler if one of them had had a boy. Corinne thought ironically, but that did not help her out of her present dilemma.

She shook her head slowly. Her light brown hair that rested on her slim shoulders gently swayed with the movement. 'I'm sorry, Clair, but I can't do it,' she said quietly.

Clair's red lips clamped together and Corinne recognised the signs only too well. 'So that's what I get for looking after you and Joy, is it?' she said in a low furious voice. 'I took you in when your grandparents died and gave you a home, and what do I get in return?' she glared at Corinne. 'Well, you'd better make the most of it, because the way things are going, I'm going to have to sell up!'

Corinne's shocked dark blue eyes met Clair's furious ones. 'You can't mean that, Clair!' she said in disbelief.

'But I do mean it!' Clair retorted, biting off the words in her fury. 'You've no idea how expensive things are. I simply must keep my London apartment, I can't possibly commute each day to work—well, I suppose I could,' she conceded grudgingly, 'but I don't see why I should have to put up with all that inconvenience, and there's certainly not enough room there for you and Joy. Not,' she added meaningly, 'that the London air would do Joy much good—not with her weak chest. Look,' she said, her voice changing to a cajoling one, 'I could look after Joy while you're out there. I can get Mrs Addle to come in and cook our meals and do the housework. You'll not be gone much above a week or two, and if it looks like hanging on—if Grandfather—well, you know what I mean—you can always say you must come home or you'll lose your job, or something like that. Just as long as you go. It's not much to ask, is it ?' she added sulkily. 'Think of Joy, she needs good country air, think of how much better she's been since you've moved into the cottage.'

Corinne did not bother to argue—not after this. Clair had meant what she had said, of that she had no doubt. It would never have occurred to her that what she had suggested was unethical, she thought bitterly, or how mean Corinne would feel about her part in the business, and for the basest of all reasons, money! She must have been stupid not to have realised it before. Clair would never have bothered to go to such lengths just to please an old man she barely knew, although he was her grandfather, even though he had ruled his family with a rod of iron, forcing his daughter to take the only way out if she wanted to marry the man of her choice and leave her home in the dead of night to put thousands of miles between her and the wrath of her father, to join her sweetheart in England and subsequently marry him.

As Clair had said, Corinne knew the story well, for in spite of the slight squabble over the christening of the girls, the families had been close. She knew that Clair's mother had rarely spoken of her old home in the Canary Islands, and only on rare occasions when Clair had exasperated her beyond reason would she comment crossly, 'You're just like your grandfather! You must have your own way, or you make life miserable for everyone!'

Corinne also knew that there had been several attempts made by Gabriel Mowbray to get his daughter to return to her home, the last one being when she lost her husband, Corinne's uncle, who had survived Corinne's parents by only a few years. That he had been able to keep tabs on his daughter after all those years, and must have had some source of information forwarded to him from England, certainly made him out to be a very formidable character, and by all accounts a wealthy one. However, Clair's mother had strongly resisted these overtures, and had said that once there, neither she nor her daughter would be able to call their lives their own, and as much as she missed the warmth and beauty of her homeland she knew that this would not compensate for the loss of freedom that she and Clair would be subjected to.

Her blunt refusal to comply with his wishes had resulted in a stony silence, and no more had been heard from him, much to the relief of Clair's mother.

On Mrs Suter's death, however, Clair's grandfather had made one other communication, this time to Clair, inviting her to visit him at any time, and that there would always be a welcome for her.

It was a letter that Clair had never replied to. She was too busy having a good time in London where she held an extremely well paid job in an advertising agency.

'How long are you going to be away?' queried Joy, later that afternoon as they sat in the small lounge where she was doing her homework, and had now done all that she was going to do.

Corinne looked up from her sewing task; she had been lengthening the skirt of Joy's new school uniform. 'Not much above a fortnight, I hope,' she replied, and bent to her task again. She had a lot of sewing to do between now and the date she was due to leave. Mrs Addle would manage the housework and the cooking, but could hardly be expected to cope with the numerous odd jobs entailed in looking after a fifteen-year-old girl.

There were seven years between Corinne and Joy, and they had lost their parents in a multiple car crash caused by fog on a four-lane highway when Corinne was ten years old and Joy only three. Corinne had not been with her parents on that fateful journey, but Joy had, and had been thrown clear at the time of the crash to lie unconscious in the thick wet grass by the side of the roadway. There had been so much confusion at the scene of the crash that the rescue teams, hampered by the fog, had not found her until quite some time after the crash.

Although she was physically unhurt, the shock of the crash had produced double pneumonia within a day or so of the accident, and had left the child with a permanently weak chest. It had not been an easy task for their grandparents, then in their early fifties, to take on the upbringing of two young girls, but they had set to the task with a will that only love can bring.

Now there was only Corinne and Joy, and Corinne jumped at Clair's offer to move into her cottage on the outskirts of a small Kentish village, referred to by Clair as 'my place in the country' to various town friends of hers. Although fully aware that behind this outwardly kind offer lay another purpose, that of having someone in residence all the year round to cope with the cleaning and tidying up of the small garden at the front and rear of the property, that had turned into a wilderness by the time Corinne and Joy moved in, Corinne had no hesitation in accepting the offer.

The built-up area of Lewisham was fine if you worked in the city, but not so good if you had the worry of a delicate girl on your hands as Corinne had, and she had snatched at the opportunity of taking Joy to the country.

'I don't see why you should go,' complained Joy, pushing her books and pen back in her satchel. 'She's got lots of London friends, hasn't she? Why can't they go for her?'

Corinne looked up at her and frowned. 'I've told you, it's a family matter, and no one else can go.' She swallowed on the thought, no one else at all. 'If Clair hadn't broken her ankle she would have gone herself—as it is—' she left the rest unsaid.

'It hasn't stopped her from enjoying herself, has it?' Joy commented with a slight moue of her pale lips. 'I thought she didn't like Ralph Patterson, but you should have heard her buttering him up when he suggested that he took her for a spin this afternoon.'

'Well, she has been stuck in for a week,' replied Corinne lamely.

'And don't we know it!' rejoined Joy smartly. 'I wish she'd go back to her London apartment, but I suppose she's got no one to look after her there and that's why she's here.' She stared at Corinne in consternation as a thought hit her. 'I say, I'm not going to wait on her hand and foot, so she needn't think I am!'

'It won't be as bad as that,' replied Corinne with a smile. 'She can get around, can't she?' The smile was replaced by a stern look. 'Do try to be a little bit helpful, Joy. We're lucky to be here, you know. We could still be living in that dismal street if Clair hadn't offered us a home here.'

'So that you could look after this place and have it ready for her to pop down with a couple of her friends whenever she feels like it!' Joy replied candidly, as she picked up her satchel. 'She doesn't do a thing about the house when she's here, you do it all. I know you don't mind, but it's the way she expects everything done for her that gets me so mad!' she declared fervently, as she made her way to the door and then turned to look at Corinne. 'You'll be back as quick as you can, won't you?' she said, with an anxious look in her grey eyes, and tossed her dark brown hair back. 'Don't worry about me, I'll be good, providing she's reasonable,' she added darkly, and left Corinne to her musings.

On the day of her departure Corinne, having spent a fretful night worrying over her coming ordeal, since she was certain that it would be an ordeal, owing to the bald fact that Clair had not bothered to even reply to her grandfather's last letter, wondered what kind of reception she would get. She would not be surprised if she was turned away at the door, and it seemed an awfully long way to go to receive what Corinne had to admit was just retribution for what could only be termed as wilful neglect on Clair's part. It would not have hurt Clair to answer the letter and thank him for his kind offer.

With these thoughts uppermost in her mind she snapped her case shut and carried it down to the lounge where Clair reclined on the settee with the telephone placed on a low table beside her, and her address book in her hand. As it was Friday, Corinne surmised she was about to ring up some friends of hers with a plea to come and relieve her boredom for the weekend.

'All packed?' she said breezily to the scowling Corinne.

Corinne gave an abrupt nod and sat down opposite

her with a determined look on her face. 'What if I'm turned away on the doorstep?' she demanded. 'Have you thought of that?'

Clair gave her a surprised look and then waved a nonchalant hand as if to refute any such possibility. 'Of course you won't be turned away,' she said lightly. 'From what Mother told me of Grandfather no one would dare go against his wishes. I imagine this Juan Martel is probably his secretary and is acting under orders.'

Corinne was not at all placated by this explanation, for it gave rise to another unpalatable thought. Suppose the old man wanted to air a few grievances, in other words, lure his granddaughter out there just to level an old score! 'I hope you won't blame me if he doesn't leave you anything,' she told Clair, practically certain that that was what Gabriel Mowbray had in mind. 'He might just want to make you think you're going to inherit and leave you nothing. Have you thought of that?' she asked her, a hopeful light coming into her eyes as she saw that her words had caused Clair a few bad moments, and the possibility that she was paying out a large sum of money on a fruitless errand began to make an impact on her.

'Nonsense!' replied Clair, although her voice did not hold much conviction. 'Get me out there just to tell me that I'm not going to get anything? Now why should he do that? His quarrel was with Mother, not with me. He wrote and asked me to visit him, remember?' she added, with more certainty.

Corinne gave her a straight look. 'And you never replied to that letter,' she reminded her accusingly.

A nonchalant shrug followed this accusation. 'I meant to,' she replied, trying unconvincingly to look rueful, 'but I never got around to it. Ah, here's your taxi! Now remember to tell him how busy I am—I mean, you are—and what a good job I've got—you've got,' she amended hastily. 'Oh, you know what I mean. I know you won't let me down. You've got a streak of sentimentality in you that will be bound to impress him.'

At seven o'clock that evening Corinne found herself sitting nervously in a handsomely furnished room that she had been led to after giving her name to the forbidding-looking woman who had admitted her to what at first appeared to be a terrace property much like many such buildings to be seen in the back street of any big city.

Once inside, however, she found herself in a different world. From where she sat in the large airy lounge she could see a garden area that appeared to be set in the middle of the house, for beyond the lit-up miniature fountain in the centre of the small garden, Corinne could see a high wall.

In spite of her nervousness, she was intrigued and longed to explore the area, but she remained where she was, particularly as she did not have Clair's faith in her expected welcome.

On her arrival in Las Palmas two hours ago, she had disobeyed Clair's orders that she should go straight to the address that she had given her, and had booked herself into an hotel for the night, as she did not want to find herself walking the streets of a strange city looking for accommodation should her gloomy predictions turn out to be correct.

The door opened suddenly and apprehensively Corinne found herself undergoing a swift but thorough scrutiny from the tall man that stood at the door. 'This way, Miss Suter,' he said abruptly. 'Your grandfather is dying. Force of will only has kept him alive until your arrival. I'm afraid he will not be able to have the talk he wanted to have with you. No matter what he says, I want you to agree to abide with his wishes. Is that clear?' he asked the stunned Corinne, who swallowed hastily and nodded. He was trying to tell her that Clair's grandfather was rambling, she thought, and would probably confuse her with Clair's mother.

Her heart was thudding against her ribs as she followed the man down a long tiled corridor and into a room at the end. He had not introduced himself, but Corinne was sure that he was the Juan Martel who had written to Clair. Her confused thoughts rambled on as she followed his tall back and was ushered into a dim-lit room. He did not look like a secretary, she thought, and hadn't acted like one either, for she had gained a fleeting impression of disdain in his voice when he had addressed her.

All this went through her mind as she adjusted her sight to the dim interior of the room and found herself looking at a gaunt man lying in a huge bed at the further end of the room.

She then felt a touch on her arm and was guided towards the bed. She steeled herself to go forward. She wanted to shout out that she was not who they thought she was and beg forgiveness from the old man who lay dying on the bed. That he was dying, she was in no doubt. His withered skin was stretched taut over his deeply hollowed cheekbones and there were large dark hollows under the beetling brows of his eyes that were closed as if in sleep.

As she watched the man who had brought her to

the room, and who now stood on the other side of the
bed, lean over and gently touch Gabriel Mowbray's
skeleton-like hand, she knew she would hold her
peace. This was no place for such disclosures. The
only salve that she could offer her conscience was
that the old man would die in peace if he thought
that his granddaughter was there.

'She's here, Gabriel,' said the man in a low clear
voice, and Corinne saw the old man's eyes open
slowly as if each movement was an effort. His blind
gaze rested first on the man who had spoken, then he
turned his gaze towards Corinne as if sensing her
presence.

'Is that you, Clair?' he whispered weakly. 'Speak,
child, for I cannot see you.'

Corinne's nails bit into her closed palms as she
forced herself to say, 'Hello, Grandfather. I came as
soon as I could.' She could not say any more. Deceiving someone who was dying was bad enough, but
ten times worse if they were blind. She wanted to
run out of that room, but her legs had turned to
wooden stumps, transfixing her where she stood.

'Bend over towards me,' whispered the weak voice
of Gabriel Mowbray.

Corinne made herself comply with this request,
wondering miserably if she was expected to kiss his
withered cheek, but he had another intention in
mind, and she held her breath as his gnarled old hand
and thin matchstick fingers went lightly over her
features, and rested for a moment on her long hair
that lay beside her cheek as she bent forward. 'Long
blonde hair like your mother,' he got out in between
a gasp. 'Not your mother's nose, though—took after
your father, eh?' There was a fit of coughing after

this, and Corinne took the opportunity to straighten up again and met the hard grey eyes of the man opposite her.

'Juan?' The name was barely audible, so weak was Gabriel Mowbray's voice. 'You know what I want. I want your word on it.'

Juan Martel's right hand reached for the hand the old man held out for him to take. 'You have my word,' he replied firmly. 'We marry, and the family will keep an interest in the business.'

The old man nodded and gave a brief grimace that Corinne took to be a smile. 'You do as Juan says, Clair,' he said weakly. 'Time you settled down and stopped gallivanti——' The word was never finished, for with a deep outward gasp Gabriel Mowbray died.

With a feeling of utter unreality Corinne watched Juan Martel draw the sheet over the still face now reposed in peace, and as if in a dream that bordered on a nightmare felt herself led to the door and through to the lounge where she had waited earlier for what seemed an eternity ago, but was in fact less than thirty minutes.

With legs that threatened to buckle under her she sat down, automatically following Juan Martel's orders, and watched him walk over to a glass cabinet and select a bottle, then with the same assured movement measure out a tot of the amber liquid into two glasses and hand one to her with an abrupt, 'Drink this. We'll talk afterwards.'

Still with a feeling of unreality, Corinne wondered what they would have to talk about. As Clair's representative she had been present at her grandfather's death, and the old man had known that she was there. She did not see what else could be expected of her. It

then occurred to her that Clair had inherited something under her grandfather's will, and that, she
thought vaguely as she sipped the strong brandy that
Juan Martel had given her, should please her.

She frowned as her bemused senses recalled the
old man's last words to her, or as he thought, to Clair,
something about it being time that she stopped galli-
vanting around, or would have said had death not
intervened.

It would appear that Clair's grandfather had kept
the same surveillance on his granddaughter as he had
had on his daughter, for there was an element of
truth in what he had said. Corinne had lost count of
the men who had occupied a brief stay in Clair's
affections, and some had been a little more than a
passing attraction, but if they were serious, it was
soon obvious that Clair was not. She was having too
good a time being wined and dined by her firm's rich
customers to tie herself down for life. The plain and
simple fact was that although rich, most of her ac-
quaintances were also married, and as she would
have put it, she had not had the luck to meet one
who was rich and eligible. Looks and love were apparently secondary considerations. Her looks alone
had guaranteed her many admirers, and she had
learnt a lot since she had successfully applied for the
job she now held. She was clever, and must have been
a great asset to the firm, not only in the mind-bending
work of the advertising profession, but the subtle
socialising that went on before a deal was clinched.

'Have you finished?' The deep voice of Juan Martel
cut into Corinne's musings, and she stared at the
empty glass in her hand, not realising that she had in
fact emptied it, and she gave a small nod and put the

glass down on a nearby occasional table.

Juan Martel studied her for a moment or two before he asked, 'Did you understand what your grandfather wanted, and what I gave him my word on?'

Corinne frowned hard in concentration trying to recall the exact wording and recalled that it had been something about marriage. He had wanted Juan Martel to marry someone and he had given his word on it. To be honest, Corinne had not taken a great deal of notice of this request since it was a personal matter between Gabriel Mowbray and the man who was now watching her so intently. She had felt bad enough just being there without listening to something that did not concern her.

She did not know what he expected her to say to this, but had an idea that perhaps he had promised to keep an eye on Gabriel's granddaughter in the future. 'I think he wanted Cl——' she coughed quickly in order to cover the slip she had almost made, 'me,' she went on, 'to settle down.' She gave him a bright smile much as Clair would have done under the same circumstances. 'He had no need to worry over me, you know. I'm quite happy as I am.' That at least was true, she thought dryly.

Her poor attempt at levity was unsuccessful, for his strong jaw hardened and his grey eyes took on an icy look. 'I see that you did not understand,' he said brusquely, 'and that I shall have to enlighten you.'

His eyes narrowed as he stared at his strong well-manicured hands before proceeding, and gave Corinne the chance to study him unobserved.

His dark hair glinted blue-black in the lighting from the small chandelier overhead, and gave Corinne the distinct impression that he was not English. Spanish perhaps, or Italian. Not that one would have known by his accent, which was perfect, and had Corinne closed her eyes and just listened to his voice, she would have been easily persuaded that he was English and very well educated, as he obviously was anyway. His features were strong and rather forbidding, and there was an autocratic look about him that many women would find fascinating. Corinne had to admit that he was what could be termed as 'good-looking' in a ruthless way, for there was a hardness about him that warned her against making a confession of her duplicity, as she had so badly wanted to do a few minutes earlier.

'I presume that you have no knowledge of your grandfather's business dealings,' Juan Martel began slowly, 'apart from the fact that he was a wealthy man,' he added, giving Corinne a sardonic smile that she did not care for at all. 'As they are rather complicated, I will simply say that he and I were partners in a hotel complex dealing solely with tourism. There were, of course, other business ventures, but as these do not concern you I will not bore you with the details,' he said brusquely. 'The hotel business, however, does concern you in as much as your grandfather wished the family to keep an interest in the business.' He looked up suddenly at Corinne's calm features. 'Surely by now you must have some idea of what was in his mind,' he said meaningly.

Corinne continued to gaze at him, but there was now puzzlement in her blue eyes. Had Gabriel Mowbray had other relations? Perhaps a sister whose daughter he wanted Juan Martel to marry? She voiced her thoughts on the matter. 'I thought that Cl—I was his only relative,' she said, cross with herself for once again almost giving herself away. This observation was made in a calm almost detached way. It was beginning to look as if there was another contender in the inheritance stakes and this would certainly not please Clair, but it did please Corinne; Clair didn't deserve to scoop up everything.

'You are,' he said flatly, and fixed a hard stare on the unsuspecting Corinne who felt that she had missed out somewhere along the line and rather wanted another rehearsal. It was then that a warning bell started clanging somewhere at the back of her mind, pealing out a message that left her speechless for several seconds. 'You mean——' she swallowed, and began again. 'You mean it was C——' Her astonishment came to her aid here, and she stared wide-eyed at the man seated opposite her who now appeared to be deriving some caustic amusement from her reaction.

'Precisely!' he said curtly, and got up from his chair and walked to the cabinet again. 'Can I get you another brandy?' he asked her dryly. 'You appear to be in need of some stimulant.'

Corinne shook her head with an emphatic movement. She needed a clear head, but more than that she desperately needed Clair's presence, but Clair was oceans away.

Her stunned gaze watched Juan pour himself out another drink and take it back with him to his chair. As before, his movements were very assured and somehow frightening. 'He couldn't expect——' began Corinne lamely, then realising that the less she said, the better it would be for her and Clair. It was Clair's problem, not hers, and broken ankle or no, she would have to take over from here on.

'Oh, yes, he could,' replied Juan, in what sounded a smug voice to Corinne, who was beginning to take a healthy dislike to him, and the way he had coldly accepted Gabriel Mowbray's dictates. It was quite obvious, she thought scathingly, that it was Clair's grandfather who really owned the business, and that this smooth character had seen a way of manipulating a few strings to gain control of the business. What a despicable man he must be, she thought hotly— agreeing to marry a girl he had not set eyes on, purely for gain. It did occur to her that he and Clair were well matched and she did wonder if this thought had occurred to the wily Gabriel Mowbray.

Her unspoken thoughts were uncannily echoed by Juan Martel as he went on smoothly, 'Gabriel had done a little homework, you see.' His cold grey eyes flicked over Corinne in a way that she highly resented. 'He was well aware of your—shall we say, somewhat disdainful attitude towards your many admirers.' He gave a twisted smile. 'We have a lot in common there, we both seek pleasure purely for pleasure's sake, but have no intention of being beholden to anyone.'

What he meant was that neither of them cared for anyone but themselves, Corinne thought scathingly, but at least he had admitted it, she conceded grudgingly. Clair had shed her boy-friends as casually as she would shed a coat, without any regard for their feelings. This man would behave in exactly the same way the moment he had lost interest in whatever poor girl he had been momentarily interested in. Oh, yes, she thought grimly, they were well matched and really deserved each other! She had to bite back the words, 'I hope you'll be very happy with each other,' and wait until she had heard the rest of it. It was obvious that he had not finished yet. She had to smother a smile at the thought of Clair's reaction to this highly enlightening interview.

'Now that we have got that part of it out of the way,' he said in a calm detached manner, 'we can discuss the marriage plans. There is quite a lot of money at stake, and there are reasons why there must be no delay in carrying out Gabriel's wishes.'

Corinne's thoughts at this juncture were not complimentary ones. Monetary reasons, she thought ironically.

'Quite apart from anything else there is a time limit, that is that we must marry within twenty-four hours of his death,' he went on smoothly. 'I gave my word on this, and do not intend to break it.'

Corinne no longer found the situation amusing. Her mind was frantically trying to find a way out for her. She must tell him the truth. It was the only thing to do. Twenty-four hours! Could Clair get there in that time? She swallowed. Yes, she could, she told herself, it was only four hours' flying time away from home. She must come if she wanted to claim her inheritance. She could hire a wheelchair, couldn't she? There had been someone on Corinne's flight who had been in the same predicament, but she had been an old lady who couldn't walk far, and they had been able to manoeuvre the chair down the narrow passageway of the plane to her seat, but Clair wouldn't have to have that done, she could hobble well enough just that short distance, so there would be no problem.

Her thoughts ran hectically on, aware the whole time of Juan Martel's close scrutiny. Just suppose she couldn't get a flight in time? 'What happens if the marriage doesn't take place?' she asked in a weak voice, as the full implication of the mess she was in hit her.

He gave an elegant shrug. 'No inheritance,' he said curtly. 'Gabriel's share of the business goes on to the open market, and there are reasons why I do not want that to happen. Our business is a competitive one and there'll be no shortage of buyers. No doubt our rivals would not be slow in moving in.' He gave her a hard stare, and as a thought occurred to him he raised his brows. 'You are not already married, are you?' he demanded.

Corinne shook her head, and he gave a satisfied nod at this. 'I didn't think Gabriel would slip up on that one,' he commented blithely, then continued in the same conversational way. 'I suggest we get it over with tomorrow morning. I would have suggested this evening, only I really think we've both had enough for one day.'

Tell him! screamed Corinne's senses, get it over with! She closed her eyes in a vain effort to compose herself, but it was useless. Her throat had gone dry, and her courage completely failed her as she realised that not only Clair would lose out on what seemed to be a substantial gain, but this hard man who had set his sights on taking over Gabriel Mowbray's business. He would very probably strangle her! She had to give Clair a chance to claim that inheritance, and somehow stall for time until she arrived. 'Can one get married, just like that?' she queried, in what she hoped was a casual voice. 'There are preparations to be made, surely?' she added on a desperate-sounding note.

Juan gave her a thin smile. 'Not in this case,' he replied slowly, studying her through narrowed eyes. 'Gabriel has had a registrar standing by. He'd got it all arranged from the moment your telegram arrived giving us your arrival date. The only thing he didn't have was time. He meant to witness our marriage before he died.'

Even in the haze of her dilemma Corinne could acknowledge this, it was typical of all that she had heard of Gabriel Mowbray. This time he was making sure that his family returned home, not only returned but stayed. He had judged Clair's character well enough to know that the golden carrot he was holding out to her would be accepted. Time, it appeared, was not the only thing Gabriel Mowbray had not had on his side; fate too, it seemed, was now putting in a strong bid to defeat him.

CHAPTER TWO

Corinne gazed down at her feet, absently taking in the mosaic pattern of the floor that told her that she was in a foreign country, where the essential ingredient for comfort was coolness during the heat of the day.

She knew that Juan Martel was awaiting her answer, and she was desperately groping for inspiration as to how she could stall for time until she could contact Clair. The same light that had brought out the blue-black lights in Juan's dark hair now gleamed on her own brown locks, and highlighted golden strands usually only visible under the rays of the sun. Her wide smooth forehead now held a frown as she searched for the answer to her problem.

She had to ring Clair; she couldn't possibly put what she had to tell her in a cablegram, and she could do nothing until she had contacted her. Was there a telephone in the house? Her worried gaze swept round the room, but as her eyes met the impatient eyes of the man still waiting for her reply she swiftly abandoned the idea. It was going to be difficult enough explaining the situation, without having him beside her or within hearing distance.

She drew a deep breath. There was nothing for it but to plead for time in giving him her answer. If the situation was hopeless there was time enough to tell him the truth, and she wanted to put this obnoxious task off for as long as possible. 'I—there are reasons why I can't give you an answer—not straight away,' she added quickly, as she saw a flash of anger in his eyes. Then she said on a note of panic, 'Getting married isn't like going out to the supermarket!' She hesitated; that had been a stupid remark, but it did convey exactly how she felt. 'What I'm trying to say is, there are other people to consider.' Not least the person who should have been sitting right where she was at that precise time! she thought cryptically.

His lips thinned into a sardonic smile. 'Where we are concerned, your description was exceedingly apt,' he replied dryly. 'I gather you want to contact someone before committing yourself? I must say,' he went on, studying her with cold disdain, 'you surprise me. This is a business arrangement; under the circumstances it can be nothing else. I'm asking nothing more from you than your signature on a marriage document. Apart from having the same outlook where our personal freedom is concerned, we have absolutely nothing in common with each other,' he added haughtily. 'I do not know how long we shall have to wait for an annulment, but I can assure you that I shall seek one at the earliest opportunity.' His cold look swept over the startled Corinne. 'I think Gabriel rather overrated our charms, and we must be thankful that he did not impose any awkward clauses, apart from marriage, in his will.'

Corinne felt the flush stain her cheeks and quickly bent her head and focused her attention on her hands tightly folded together in her lap. She was very well aware of his meaning, and he must have had a shock when he had first seen her. He had been expecting a beauty and had found himself staring at a mousy, nondescript girl. She swallowed. No wonder he was anxious to obtain an annulment! She wondered what his reaction would have been if Clair had come as she should have done, and was certain that his attitude would have been an entirely different one.

Here again she was forced to agree with old Gabriel's reasoning. Juan Martel was a very attractive man. Corinne did not like him, but she had to acknowledge this, and knew instinctively that Clair would have been very interested in him—still would be, she thought musingly, if she could get a flight out there.

Clair's blonde beauty and Juan Martel's dark good looks would go well together, quite apart from the fact that they were both fortune-seekers as well as pleasure-seekers. This thought made her feel a little better, for his bald comments, no matter how obliquely put, had hurt her, and she couldn't understand why. She was not normally apt to take offence at such remarks, not that any had been made in the past, and if they had, she would have shrugged them off with an amused smile.

Corinne was not aware of the fact that there were different grades of beauty, and that she was well qualified to claim a place in the grading. She had not noticed that though Clair would invariably draw the immediate notice of the male sex, it was herself who received the longer look. There was a quality about her and a serenity that was both attractive and appealing to the opposite sex. She certainly did not come under the nondescript label that she had given herself.

Her finely shaped arched brows, that were nature's gift and owed nothing to beauty aids, and her wide dark blue eyes that expressed her feelings so clearly, placed her far above the low rating she had attached to herself. Her short, straight nose, that Gabriel had remarked upon, and in which he had been perfectly correct, for Clair had inherited her mother's classical features, emphasised Corinne's femininity. A wide generous mouth set in a heartshaped face completed a picture that was entirely pleasing to the eye, as even the fastidious Juan Martel would have acknowledged.

'I regret, however, that we do not possess a telephone,' Juan said, after the short pause that had followed his last rather cutting remarks. 'Gabriel refused to have one installed here, insisting on a modicum of peace in his home—but that is beside the point. I do know of a public booth that you could use.' He stood up at this point. 'As I need to know your answer tonight, I shall escort you there.'

After the first quick flow of relief that Corinne had felt at this helpful attitude of Juan Martel, she wondered if he realised that she would be ringing someone in England, and not someone in Las Palmas. She gave him an apologetic look as she got up from her chair. 'Thank you,' she said gravely. 'It's not a local call, you understand, so perhaps the hotel——'

He gave a curt nod as he ushered her to the door. 'I had gathered that,' he replied coldly, and gave her a hard stare. 'I wondered why you had no luggage with you. You booked into an hotel, did you?'

Corinne looked away from his cold stare. She ought to have done what Clair had told her to do and gone straight to the address she had given her. 'I wasn't sure that'—she hesitated—'Grandfather could put me up,' she added lamely.

'You have forgotten a lot about your family, haven't you?' he said on an icy note, then added thoughtfully, 'Perhaps that explains a lot, but it hardly compensates.'

He said no more, but Corinne had a nasty feeling that she knew exactly what was behind this remark. Clair might have made an effort to visit her grandfather; she hadn't even had the excuse of not being able to afford to, as all her expenses would have been paid.

She followed the haughty back of Juan Martel out of the house, and a little way along the road until he stopped beside a heavy studded double door and producing a key, opened the doors to reveal a garage which housed an expensive-looking car. Corinne's brows rose slightly as she noted the Mercedes crest on the front of the car. If the car was a status symbol, and they usually were, then whatever share Juan

Martel held in Gabriel Mowbray's business, it was a profitable one, she thought.

'Which hotel have you booked into?' he asked her, as the sleek car cruised out of the side street into the main street.

Corinne gave him the name, mentioning that it was on the sea-front and not too far away, to which he gave another of those curt nods of his and said that he knew where it was, and that in fact the telephone box that he had in mind was only a few yards outside the hotel. He had then given her another of those quick hard looks of his and said, 'You could probably phone from the hotel, but there would not be much privacy, as you would have to use the switchboard. I gather you would prefer a little privacy?'

Until now Corinne had managed to thrust the thought of talking to Clair and trying to explain the position in what short time she would have out of her mind, but now she was forced to face it. She didn't quite know how she was going to get on with this frigid man probably leaning against the panels of the telephone box while he waited for her to make the call. That was bad enough without having to contend with an interested switchboard operator avidly listening to the conversation! 'Thank you, yes, I would prefer privacy,' she replied through dry lips, praying that he would not offer to escort her to the phone booth.

The evening traffic was very heavy, and they were held up several times on the way, but Corinne was grateful for this. She needed as much time as she could get before talking to Clair. Time to rehearse what she had to say so that Clair understood the

position. That was surely plain enough; she had to
get a flight out there right away or she would lose
her inheritance. She couldn't blame Corinne if she
lost everything, which she very probably would, she
thought despondently. Corinne had had to wait for
a cancellation before she had been able to make the
journey, but she had been lucky and had got one
within a week. How could Clair possibly get a flight
within twenty-four hours? Corinne asked herself
miserably, as the vision of Joy and herself tramping
the streets looking for accommodation rose like a
spectre in front of her.

'So someone got through at last, did they?' asked
Juan, breaking into Corinne's miserable musings.
'And that's a surprise too, but I gather he won't mind
waiting until the annulment?' He flashed her a quick
look. 'Unless he can provide you with enough money
to keep you solvent, I presume he will have to. You're
in debt, aren't you?' he stated flatly.

Startled, Corinne stared at him, and it took a moment or two to get the gist of what he was saying.
He obviously thought that it was a man that she
wanted to get in touch with. As for Clair being in
debt, that did not surprise her, but the fact that this
smooth character was aware of this did surprise her.
She gazed out at the lighted shopping area they were
passing and felt a surge of hopelessness flow over her.
It was becoming increasingly obvious that Clair had
been well aware that her grandfather was a wealthy
man. She had run through the substantial legacy her
mother had left her in an amazingly short time to
Corinne's way of thinking, for Corinne had had no
idea that she was short of money until Clair had
given her the ultimatum of going to Las Palmas in her

place, or losing the home she had provided for her and Joy.

It was typical of Clair to leave things to the last moment, and it would not have occurred to her that her grandfather would have imposed any clauses on her inheritance. All she had to do was to turn up at the right time, armed with what she thought would be valid excuses as to why she had not been able to visit him in the past, and charm her way back into his affections. It would have worked too, Corinne thought miserably, only like her grandfather's hopes, fate had intervened, and her well-laid plans had been disrupted by a broken ankle, an injury she had incurred while pursuing her favourite sport of ice skating.

Corinne moved restlessly in the soft leather seat of the car. She might as well tell Juan Martel to stop the car somewhere and tell him everything. She didn't care what he thought of her or Clair. It really served them both right. She was as much to blame as Clair was; she ought never to have come. Clair would be even more in debt now, having paid out for the fare for what was a completely fruitless journey, and she wondered if the sale of the cottage would free her from debt.

The man beside her took her silence as confirmation, and went on in that hateful smooth voice of his, 'I do hope he sees reason for both our sakes.'

Corinne continued to look out of the window. She could not answer him. She did not know enough about Clair's affairs to argue the point. In any case, his supposition that there was a man in the background was not correct. Clair was not likely to make a mistake like that, not unless she had genuinely fallen in love, and however close she had been about her financial affairs, Corinne would have heard about that.

The road they were now cruising down looked vaguely familiar to Corinne, and when Juan guided the car into a parking space, she could see the sea ahead of her and got her bearings, for the hotel she had booked into was just around the corner of the street facing the promenade, and this was as far as the car could go.

For an agonising moment she wavered as to whether to confess all then and there, but her courage completely failed her as she looked at the cold profile of the man beside her. She would speak to Clair first, she told herself, trying to calm her taut nerves. If she could give him some hope that Clair would make an effort to put in an appearance before the deadline, he just might not strangle her, she thought miserably as she got out of the car.

'The box is on the right,' Juan said brusquely, as they walked towards the sea-front, and so it was, Corinne saw, and it was mercifully empty although there were many people strolling along the promenade. 'I'll be over there,' he said, indicating a café a short way along the promenade that had several tables out on the promenade.

Corinne nodded and walked towards the box. Her thankfulness that Juan Martel would not be within hearing distance of her conversation with Clair was soon engulfed by her anxiety to talk to Clair.

It took a tensed-up moment to read the directions and fumble for the amount required, thankful that she had some change from a note that she had given the taxi driver who had brought her from the airport

to the hotel. It was as well for Corinne that she
had made a point of learning the currency before coming to Las Palmas, but even so she found time to
wonder at the cheapness of the call, considering the
distance involved.

'Clair must come,' she muttered to herself, as she
dialled the number, praying that she was in because one
never knew with Clair. As Joy had said, her injury had
not stopped her from enjoying herself.

A quick glance at her watch as she heard the buzzing
tone at the other end of the line told her that it was just
on nine o'clock, and that meant that it was only ten
o'clock at home.

'Faversham four-one-two,' Clair's voice came calmly
over the line to the strung-up Corinne, who gave a quick
gasp of relief and immediately forgot her well-rehearsed
wording.

'Clair? Oh, thank goodness! I've got to marry him,
and I can't, can I?' she babbled out frantically. 'You've
got to come out here. Hire a wheelchair or something—
but come!' she urged frantically.

'Marry my grandfather!' exclaimed Clair. 'For
goodness' sake, what's happened? Has he found you
out?'

Corinne clenched the telephone receiver hard.
'Not your grandfather—Juan Martel! You know, the
one who wrote to you! Oh, damn, there go the bleeps
and I don't think I've got another fifty pesetas, hang
on while I look—don't you dare go away!' she
threatened, as she hunted for the necessary coin and
finding one pushed it in the slot provided before the
call was finished. 'Clair? For goodness' sake, what
shall I do? He'll have to know the truth, won't he?
Clair? You're still there, aren't you?' she demanded,

in the small silence that followed.

'Of course I'm still here,' replied Clair. 'Now calm down and tell me what's happened.'

Corinne took a deep breath and swallowed the impulse to scream out the latest developments. She must keep calm and make Clair understand the position. 'He promised your grandfather that he'd marry you. He's his partner, you see, but he's not going to go through with it all—I mean, he wants to keep his promise, but that's as far as he wants to go. He says he'll get an annulment later. If you don't marry, he can't divide the property, it's in the will, you see, and it's got to be done within twenty-four hours. You've got to get here somehow!' she wailed.

'That's out of the question,' replied Clair irritably. 'I gather Grandfather died?' she asked abruptly, then before Corinne could confirm this she went on to say peevishly, 'I might have known he'd something like this in mind.'

'Well, that's that,' said Corinne despondently. 'I'd better come home.'

'You stay right where you are,' Clair replied sharply. 'I'm not that easily defeated, and I need that money.' There was silence for a few seconds, then Clair said excitely, 'Wait! There is a way it can be done—you've heard of marriage by proxy, haven't you? I don't know all the ins and outs of it, but I'm pretty sure it will work. It's got to!' she muttered half to herself. 'Look, I'll get on to a friend of mine, he handles the firm's legal work, he'll know what has to be done. I've an idea that all that's required is a document signed by me authorising you as a stand-in at the marriage. If it can't be done I'll contact you at Grandfather's.'

Corinne's frantic, 'There won't be time, Clair, he wants the marriage to take place tomorrow morning,' was met with a firm, 'Well, stall him until the afternoon, he won't mind a few hours' delay when you tell him the reason. He stands to gain as much as I do.'

Corinne's quick, 'But I'm not staying at your grandfather's,' was not quick enough, for Clair had hung up on her, leaving her staring at the silent instrument in her hand, and she stayed like that until an insistent knocking on the panel of the phone box reminded her that someone was waiting to make a call.

It took all Corinne's will power to step out of that phone box and turn her lagging steps towards the café where Juan Martel was waiting for her. Only a few yards the other way was the hotel that she had booked into and would give her sanctuary she was sure she was going to need after she had made her confession, and she was grateful for the fact that it was within walking distance!

CHAPTER THREE

JUAN MARTEL stood up as she approached him, and there must have been something in Corinne's expression that alerted him to the fact that all was not well, although Corinne had assumed what she hoped was a bland expression.

His harsh, 'Well?' sounded very ominous to the over-sensitive Corinne, and she gave a swift glance around them wondering if it were possible to have

what promised to be a nerve-racking session over a
cup of coffee at the table he stood beside.

The arrival of a merry party of tourists who took
the next table to his finally decided her. 'I have to
talk to you,' she said quietly, adding in a low voice,
'but not here.'

His dark brows rose at this, but he gave a curt nod
and looked towards the hotel across the way where
Corinne had booked in on her arrival. 'We shall take
advantage of their lounge,' he said abruptly. 'Most of
the guests will be enjoying an evening stroll by now.'

To Corinne's vast relief his presumption proved
correct, and the large lounge, well provided with
ample seating in the form of dark leather club chairs
grouped around tables, was practically empty apart
from a couple at the further end of the room enjoying
an after-dinner coffee.

As Corinne seated herself in a deep comfortable
chair placed against the lounge window that looked
out on to the sea, she had no time to admire the view,
that in the daytime would no doubt be a splendid
one, but now at night had its own romantic charm,
for further along the shore on the promenade that
skirted the length of the sea-front, lamps had been lit,
giving a fairytale effect to the whole area.

The area might as well have been clothed in thick
fog for all the effect it had on Corinne, who was
desperately trying to assemble her thoughts in order
to present the bare unpalatable truth to this hawk-
eyed man sitting opposite her, and whose strong lean
fingers had just switched on the lamp on the table beside her, making her feel as if she was about to under-
go some sort of third degree, and in all probability
she was, she thought miserably.

She gave him a quick nervous glance, and noting the way the shadows around him seemed to highlight his harsh features, she swallowed before saying, 'You're not going to like this.'

She saw him stiffen and noted the quick flash of fury in his cold eyes. 'I gave my word,' he said haughtily, 'and my word's my bond. The marriage will be annulled at the earliest possible time. Your grandfather was well aware of this possibility,' he gave a thin smile. 'As I believe I mentioned earlier, he was under the mistaken impression that in spite of my dedicated stand against matrimony, we should find that we had a lot in common. Happily for both of us he was so sure of this conviction that he made no stipulation other than that we should marry. Your man can rest assured that as soon as I have your signature on the marriage document you will be free to return home. No other obligation is required of you.'

'It's not that,' Corinne replied quickly, wanting to get the confession over with before she was exposed to another cold directive as to her failure to come up to the beauty standard likely to attract his fastidious palate in the romantic stakes. 'I'm not Clair Suter—at least, I am, but not the Clair Suter you were expecting,' she got out on a rush of words, hardly pausing for breath, and experienced a vast wave of relief as if a load had suddenly been removed from her slim shoulders.

Hardly daring to look at him, she darted a quick glance up at him to watch his reaction, and it was much as expected. His hooded eyes were fixed on her and if he had appeared cold before, he was positively icy now. 'Would you mind being a little more explicit?' he queried, in a silky voice that made Corinne quake inside.

'I'm Clair's cousin,' she said, trying to ignore the warning glints in his eyes. 'She broke her ankle, you see, and couldn't come, and rather than disappoint——' she ended the sentence too lamely, and she knew it, but couldn't do anything about it. It was bad enough making the confession without belabouring the point as to why such a deception had been necessary.

'Rather than lose out on her inheritance, you mean, don't you?' he queried harshly. 'There's no need to wrap it up, I've got the picture.' His disdainful look swept over Corinne and she felt a flush stain her cheeks; she could guess his thoughts only too well. 'And what do you have to gain by being her accomplice?' he asked. 'A share in the proceeds? That would be it, of course. As for you being another Clair Suter, you might give me credit for some intelligence,' he added harshly. 'Were you willing to perjure yourself on that too?' He gave her a speculating look. 'You could have gone ahead with the marriage on that premise, couldn't you? What happened? Did your courage fail you at the last moment?' He stared down at his hands now clenched on the table and Corinne had a feeling he was finding it hard keeping them off her.

'On second thoughts, no,' he went on, reverting back to the silky tone. 'You had to get further instructions, didn't you? What a shock you must have given her!' He sat back and folded his hands across his chest. 'Well?' he queried, almost conversationally. 'What instructions did you receive? I can't quite see her giving up at this stage. She went to a lot of

trouble to cash in on Gabriel's demise. Will she contest the will, I wonder? I can quite understand why
she baulked at your signing the marriage certificate,
particularly if you do happen to bear the same name.
She couldn't afford to trust you that far, could she?
So, however improbable it sounds, you could be
right about that. However, you must forgive me for
not taking your word on this. I presume you have
some form of identification on you?'

Corinne gave a stiff nod and searched in her handbag for her passport, and finding it, she handed it to
him, saying, 'I told you the truth.' She could have
added a lot more to this as she was beginning to feel
that she had reached the limit of what she was prepared to take from this hateful character. What right
had he to condemn Clair? He was just as interested
in Gabriel Mowbray's money as Clair was.

He took his time in examining the passport, then
handed it back to her in cold silence, and refolded
his arms across his chest in an action that said more
than words, reminding Corinne that there was another question that he had asked regarding Clair's
answer to her telephone call, and was still waiting
for her reply.

Corinne forced herself not to lose her temper. She
knew she deserved the treatment she was receiving,
and would willingly have accepted the medicine had
not the man in question been so infuriatingly sure
of himself. With anyone else, she might have apolo-
gised for her part in the deception, but not to this
man, who would only have seen such an apology as
a ploy to gain his sympathy, for goodness knows
what, she thought crossly. 'Clair said something
about marriage by proxy,' she said stiffly. 'She

seemed to think it was possible, and that all that was required was a signed letter giving me the authority to act for her——'

Juan Martel did not give her time to complete the sentence in which she was about to add her sentiments on the matter, and that she was sure that such an arrangement was a forlorn hope, but that she had tried. 'Did you tell her of the time factor?' he demanded.

Corinne gave him a cold look. Like Clair, he was prepared to snatch at any opportunity that offered itself in order to claim his proceeds from the will, even such an unlikely opportunity as marriage by proxy. 'Of course,' she replied, with as much hauteur as she could manage, 'but under the circumstances, I hardly think——'

Again she was interrupted by the forceful Juan who was obviously not interested in her observations. 'What a resourceful woman,' he remarked thoughtfully, 'Gabriel would have been proud of her.'

Corinne stared at him. He was acting as if such a thing was possible, but it couldn't be! she thought wildly, she didn't want it to be possible. She wanted this man to lose out, Clair too; neither deserved to win. So she would have to find another home for herself and Joy, but by now she had become quite used to the idea. She was good at housekeeping, and there were always people advertising for such help. She stole a look at the man opposite her and found him studying her as if she were an interesting specimen he had chanced upon. He didn't look as if he had lost out, in fact, he looked immensely pleased with himself, and felt a pang of unease. 'You mean, it is possible?' she asked, almost holding her breath for the answer.

'Oh, yes,' he replied blandly. 'I have no doubt at all that she will do all that has to be done. I could, of course, refuse to accept such an arrangement, but as it happens, it suits me perfectly.' His cold eyes travelled slowly over Corinne as he said this, and she felt a warning flash somewhere at the back of her brain, but immediately dismissed it. She knew she was very strung-up and it was no small wonder after what she had been through that evening. Her apprehension could be attributed entirely to an emotional backlash.

Clair would make sure that the necessary documents arrived in time, and if they didn't—well—she had nothing to worry about. She would book the earliest possible flight home. The shores of old England would look like the Taj Mahal in moonlight to the weary Corinne at that moment in time.

A waiter then hovered beside their table and enquired whether they wanted any refreshment, and Juan looked at Corinne, who was about to refuse, but at his, 'I rather think we have cause to celebrate, don't you?' was forced to change her mind and asked for a mint-julep, although a double brandy would have been more in keeping with events!

It was amazing, she thought ironically, how relaxed and charming Juan Martel had become now that his hopes had been realised. He must have been really counting on inheriting his partner's share in the business, and she wondered caustically if he were in debt too. Her assessing eyes swept over his immaculate dark suit that fitted him so perfectly, and on to his white silk shirt. He represented a picture of a successful man, but looks could be misleading, she thought sourly, and in this case surely were.

When the drinks had been served Juan held his glass of brandy up towards her in a salutory action and said, 'Here's to the wedding.' Corinne's hand stayed on her glass and she did not echo his sentiments, but gave what she hoped was an understanding smile only it did not reach her eyes.

Her refusal to enter into the spirit of celebration obviously piqued the autocratic Juan, who began to ask her a few questions that she would rather not have to reply to. She could not be absolutely sure, but she suspected that this was his way of punishing her for her lack of response to his toast.

The first was not too hard to deal with. He was curious about the name coincidence of the cousins, and she told him that it was no coincidence, and gave him a short résumé of the family history.

The next question was the one that she had been dreading. What sort of a job did she have? and had she given it up on presumption of the reward she would receive for services given?

By this time Corinne was convinced that he was punishing her, and her answers were short and very much to the point. She did not embroider on the fact that she had only a part-time job, he could think what he liked about that. As for the reward he thought she was hoping to collect, she told him that it would be adequate for her needs, thank you, and sat back in cold silence waiting for the next question.

Now that she knew that he was out to rile her, she was able to keep a tight rein on her temper and not give him the satisfaction of piercing through her defences, but his next question threw her out of her complacency. 'Why did you agree to do as she asked?' he queried softly, his narrowed gaze searching her dark blue eyes now opened wide in surprise, and then taking in the bright pink flush that stained her flawless complexion.

The question stunned her for a second, then she made a swift recovery and gave a casual shrug much as Clair would have done when faced with a problem that she did not feel warranted her attention. 'It seemed a good idea,' she replied, as nonchalantly as she was able.

'Are you in debt?' he asked suddenly.

Corinne shook her head emphatically, and her eyes showed her indignation at the question. 'Of course not!' she replied, as if the very idea was unthinkable.

Her reply seemed to substantiate his thoughts on the matter, and he gave her a piercing look. 'What hold does she have on you then?' he queried harshly.

'No hold at all!' Corinne spat out at him. 'And even if she had, I wouldn't tell you. You've no right to ask such questions!'

'So it was a kind of blackmail,' he mused thoughtfully.

'It was not blackmail either,' she got out, hating the way he had cornered her with just a few pointed questions. 'I wanted to help her,' she went on in a low voice, refusing to meet his searching eyes. Then suddenly she was sick of the whole business. She could see his reasoning; he knew quite a lot about Claire, obviously from her grandfather. It was also obvious that he had not been enamoured by her exploits. That he thought her capable of using blackmail to gain Corinne's co-operation came as a slight shock to Corinne. Yet in a way he had not been all that far off the mark; it had been a subtle kind of blackmail that had been used.

'I—she's been very good to me and Joy,' she went on slowly, wanting to get it all over with so that she could be left in peace. 'She provided us with a home. She has a cottage in the country——' She broke off suddenly, as she realised that if she went on Juan would soon know the reason why she had agreed to take her place in Las Palmas.

'That she threatened to sell,' Juan finished for her, with an accuracy that took Corinne's breath away, and she wondered why she had bothered to try and hide the truth from him.

The conversation was beginning to get a little out of hand, and Corinne was very tired. She stood up with a determined air. 'If you don't mind, I'm very tired,' she said coldly. 'It's been a long day for me.'

Juan's expressive brows rose at this, but he stood up immediately. 'My apologies,' he said quietly. 'Will ten o'clock tomorrow suit you?'

Corinne stared at him, then blinked swiftly. He was referring to the marriage, of course. 'But Clair won't have got her authorisation over here as early as that,' she protested. 'Wouldn't it be better to put it off until later?' she suggested, with a hint of panic in her voice at the very thought of standing next to this forceful man and exchanging the marriage vows even though she was only standing in for Clair.

Juan Martel gave her a long hard look before he said firmly, 'The registrar is a very busy man, and I have already made the arrangements. I do not envisage any hold-up. I shall collect you at nine-thirty. Please be ready. I have a lot of arrangements to make afterwards.'

The last remark was uttered as a cold directive, and Corinne was again reminded of his forcefulness. She knew there was no point in arguing, it would be like coming up against a stone wall. It would serve him right, she thought furiously, if Clair was unable to get the documentation through in time! However, she said nothing, but gave a small swift nod in reply before she wished him a stiff-sounding 'Good-night,' and left the lounge to collect her keys from the hotel desk.

When she reached her room, she found that her hand was trembling as she fumbled with the key to let herself in, and as soon as she was in the room she locked the door after her.

On legs that felt like rubber she walked over to the single divan and threw her handbag down on it, then slowly sat down on the bed. Her thoughts were chaotic, but above all was the intense desire to sleep, and she prepared herself for bed.

It was not until she was under the shower in the bathroom that she remembered what Clair had said about contacting her if her plan was not going to work. Corinne's small teeth clamped on to her lower lip as she toyed with the idea of ringing Clair again, this time from the hotel, as the message would not be quite such a personal one, and giving her the hotel number to ring if things went wrong.

By the time she had emerged from the shower, however, she had changed her mind. The chances were that Clair was already burning up the wires from Kent to wherever the legal man she had mentioned lived, and would not take kindly to another call from Corinne. It was not as if her message to Las Palmas would be wasted. Juan Martel would be sure to receive any message of that importance, for Corinne was certain he would be staying at Clair's grandfather's house to complete the arrangements that he had spoken of, the funeral arrangements being the first and foremost.

When Corinne climbed thankfully into the bed, she wondered if Clair would put herself out to attend the funeral, and thought that perhaps she would. She would have to meet her grandfather's partner some time, who would by that time be her husband, even though it was only a business arrangement. There would be a lot they would have to discuss, she thought tiredly as she slipped in between the cool sheets. She wondered too what Clair would make of her newly acquired husband, and gave an ironical smile. Somehow she could not see her being in too much of a hurry to return to England—or looking forward to the annulment! Old Gabriel Mowbray had sized up the situation with a well practised eye. Corinne knew Clair, and now she knew Juan Martel, and they might have been made for each other!

Corinne did not remember much after her head had touched the pillow, and she slept right through until the morning, when the rays of the sun pierced through a chink in the curtains of the french windows that led out on to a small balcony facing the sea.

After she had first opened her eyes, it took her a moment or two to get her bearings, and when she had them she sat up in bed with a jerk and reached for her wristwatch on the bedside table with a nasty feeling that she had overslept, and that at any moment she would hear pounding on the bedroom door and a furious Juan Martel demanding to know what was keeping her.

The hands of the watch pointed to eight o'clock, and Corinne sank back in bed with a sigh of relief. She had a full hour and a half before the arrival of the indomitable Juan Martel.

Corinne got down to breakfast just before eight-thirty, and found herself joining a straggling line lined up beside a long buffet table that ran the length of the dining room. There was not a waiter in sight, but the loaded table provided an adequate breakfast on continental lines.

There were soft sweet rolls, or crisp plain rolls beside small dishes that held wrapped butter portions, and small pots of marmalade or various other jams according to taste. A little further up the table were large plates of sliced ham, and wafer-thin processed cheese slices, and what looked like some kind of seasoned sausage slices. Of the traditional eggs and bacon there was no sign, but such fare could have been had, Corinne found, as she progressed down the line and saw someone ring a bell for attention from the kitchen staff and give an order. Corinne, however, was well satisfied with a crisp roll and a pot of marmalade, and pouring herself a cup of coffee from one of the two urns at the end of the line, she carried her tray over to a table near the window that looked out on to the promenade.

While she ate her breakfast, she watched the other guests come and go. As it was early, there was not a rush for the tables with the best view, and she was left in peace to finish her meal without the necessity of making small conversation.

The gay chatter and expectancy of the day ahead

proclaimed the other guests to be tourists, and Corinne surmised that she was the only person there on a business trip. The various modes of dress verified this, although she did feel it was going a little too far to appear in one's dressing gown, as an elderly lady wrapped in a long towelled arrangement joined the queue.

Although the sea had a misty look about it, all the signs promised a warm day, and Corinne, recalling that it was early March and there had been a bitter wind at home, in spite of the small green shoots of the early flowering bulbs cautiously poking out of the hard ground, gave a small sigh. How wonderful it would have been if she had been there on holiday with Joy.

These thoughts depressed her, and she turned her attention to the other guests again. From what she could hear of the conversations around her, most of them were English, with a smattering of Continentals, for she heard what she thought was German from a couple at the next table to hers, the man very correctly dressed in a blue short-sleeved shirt and tailored shorts, the woman with a pink blouse with a gypsy styled top and wide floral skirt.

Corinne's cream sleeveless dress did not look at all out of place in such a gathering, but it did occur to her that the autocratic Juan Martel might not think the dress at all suitable for the occasion, and that perhaps she ought to change into the blue and white suit that she had brought with her. It would certainly be more in keeping with the proposed wedding arrangements, although she would personally have preferred to wear a dress that she felt more comfortable in.

It was shortly before nine when she went back to her room to change into the suit. She slipped off the dress and put on the skirt of the suit, which was cut plain and straight, and then put on the white tie-neck blouse, wondering whether to make a bow of the tie or leave it folded over. After trying out the bow effect, she decided that she did not like it that way. It looked a little too frivolous for her liking, and she undid the bow and left it folded over. The jacket was the box style and fitted snugly to her slim figure. It had white piping on the edge of the sleeves and on the imitation pockets.

Her high-heeled navy blue court shoes completed the ensemble, and she stood back to survey the finished result, then gave a swift nod of approval, and then a slight smile, for it was fitting that she should wear one of Clair's cast-offs for the occasion.

The girls were the same size, and whenever Clair had become tired of a particular article of clothing she would pass it on to Corinne. As Corinne's taste was of a much simpler nature than Clair's, this was not always appreciated by Corinne, but she would endeavour to look suitably grateful and then thrust it away at the back of her wardrobe.

This suit, however, had been an exception, it had been too plain for Clair, and she had passed it on to Corinne with the remark that she couldn't think what possessed her to buy it. It had been Clair who had suggested that she take the suit with her. She had kept a wary eye on Corinne's packing, aware of the fact that Corinne was her representative.

A glance at her watch told her that she had only ten minutes to await the arrival of Juan Martel, and she decided to go down to the lounge to wait for him.

It was only as she was leaving her room that the thought occurred to her that she did not possess a hat, and she stood frowning in the middle of her room wondering whether it was permissible to remain bareheaded. With a sigh of exasperation she turned back to her suitcase and searched for a blue and white polka-dot scarf that she had brought with her, and hastily tied it round her hair, bandeau-style. It was the best she could do under the circumstances, she thought crossly. She had not expected to find herself standing in for a bride.

It was clear from the swift appreciative look that she received from Juan Martel on his arrival that her appearance pleased him, although he made no comment.

His own apparel was fully in keeping with the proceedings and Corinne noted the way several female heads were turned in his direction as he entered the hotel, for she had waited for him in the hotel lobby. His well-cut dark grey pinstripe suit sat snugly on his broad shoulders, and his silk shirt with the pearl grey tie would not have looked out of place at Ascot on Ladies' Day. All that was missing was the top hat worn by the sporting gentlemen on such an occasion, Corinne thought, as she watched him approach.

As he escorted her to his car, drawn up as before around the corner from the hotel, Corinne found herself thinking how Clair would have hated missing out on this stage of the proceedings.

When the car's engine purred into life, Corinne darted a swift look at the silent man beside her and asked, 'Any word from Clair?' which was a stupid thing to ask, she thought afterwards, because if Clair had contacted him she would not be on the way to the registrar, and she was not surprised when he did not deign to answer but just lifted those expressive dark brows of his.

The ceremony was conducted in Spanish, and after a few forceful prompts from Juan, Corinne gave the appropriate replies. It was all over in what seemed a matter of minutes, and Corinne felt better about the whole thing. She had never attended a register office wedding before, but she had heard of how quick the ceremony was, and how hard it had been for the participants to actually realise that they were indeed married.

When she had placed her signature on the record, and received a hearty handshake from the small genial registrar, she breathed out a sigh of relief. She had done all that had been required of her and she was now free to go home, and hoped she would not have to wait too long for a flight.

Her mind was concentrating on such mundane things as buying a small present for Joy, and she supposed she ought to get Clair something too, when Juan, escorting her out of the register office, suggested that they take an early lunch as they had a lot to get through that day.

Corinne's surprised look rested on Juan, and she thought it was kind of him to want to take her to lunch, but surely he would want to get on and not be encumbered by her presence? She voiced these thoughts as tactfully as possible, ending with, 'I can get a snack back at the hotel.'

Juan gave her a small hard smile. 'We've a lot to talk about, and arrangements to make. I have asked Maria to have lunch waiting for us on our return.'

Corinne frowned at this. He was taking a lot for

granted, she thought, as she allowed herself to be taken back to his car.

On the way back to Gabriel's house, Corinne tried to work out what he had meant by their having a lot to talk about, and when the answer came she chided herself for her stupidity. He would want to explain the intricacies of the partnership to her so that she could report back to Clair—also the amount which Clair would be inheriting. Clair would have been furious with her if she had not verified this most important aspect of the will for her.

Clair ought to have made the effort to come over, she thought crossly, and then she remembered the funeral. 'I'm sure Clair will try to come for the funeral,' she said quickly, then added lamely, 'If she can get a flight, that is,' and stole a swift glance at the cold handsome profile of the man beside her, who appeared to be not the least interested in his new bride's future plans.

Corinne looked away and studied the teeming traffic around them. Well, of course he couldn't be expected to be, she thought soberly. He had said that he had no interest in her apart from wanting her co-operation in fulfilling the terms of Gabriel Mowbray's will.

The journey did not take long, and soon they were drawing up outside the double doors of the garage.

While Juan garaged the car Corinne waited outside the garage. It did occur to her that he could have left the car outside the house as she did not anticipate staying long after the proposed lunch, during which she presumed he would outline the main points of the will to her.

They were admitted by the same dour-looking

woman whose expression lightened considerably on
sight of Juan Martel, and she answered the questions
he asked of her with an almost eager attempt to
please.

Corinne could not understand what had been said,
and even if she had had a spattering of Spanish she
would not have been able to follow the conversation,
they had spoken so rapidly.

Juan then led her to a cool, spacious dining-room,
and Corinne saw that the table was laid ready for
lunch with an assortment of food temptingly laid
out on the white damask cloth. Great care had been
taken to provide the meal, and Corinne felt very
embarrassed as her gaze took in the plates of de-
licious-looking pastries, a dish of huge prawns, and
several other dishes to tempt the appetite. If Maria,
as Juan had called the housekeeper, had known of
the impromptu wedding, she could not have provided
better fare for the wedding breakfast, she thought
confusedly, and wondered how much Maria did
know.

As soon as they were seated, Maria bustled in
carrying a large silver tray with matching coffee jug
and delicately engraved cups and saucers, which she
placed on a large ornamental sideboard that gleamed
with countless polishings. Then she turned and
nodded to Corinne in a way that suggested that she
was pleased to be of service to her, and left the dining
room.

Now that she was completely alone with the man
who had just married Clair, Corinne's embarrassment
was heightened, and this annoyed her. She reminded
herself that she had no need to feel embarrassed. As
distasteful as the whole thing was, it was a business

arrangement, and she was only a go-between being treated to lunch at the management's expense. Therefore she ought to at least enjoy it, she argued silently with herself. She felt much better after this, and when Juan offered her the dish of prawns she realised that she was hungry after all, and began to enjoy the lunch.

When no mention of business had been made by the time they reached the coffee stage, Corinne wondered when Juan would broach the subject, and presumed that he was waiting until lunch was over.

As she accepted the coffee that he had just poured out for her, she felt a pang of regret that this pleasant interlude would soon be over. Under Juan's skilful handling she had lost all trace of embarrassment. He had kept her well entertained during lunch on the various aspects of running a luxury hotel. There was no such thing as an off-season, and the hotel was fully booked all the year round owing to the pleasant Canarian climate, and Corinne was reminded of the earlier names given to the islands by the seafarers of old, such as 'the Fortunate Islands' —or 'the Blessed Islands'.

Until that morning Corinne had only seen one side of Juan Martel; now she was seeing another, a charming and exceedingly attractive side of the man who had been Gabriel Mowbray's partner. It was perhaps as well for Corinne that she was fully aware of the danger of losing her heart to this undeniably handsome man, whose very knowing grey eyes could hold either a challenge or a chilling rebuke without a word being spoken.

It was also as well that she was aware of the determination that lay behind that lazy smile of his to get what he wanted out of life, and she pitied any woman unlucky enough to get embroiled with him. Her first thought that he and Clair were well matched had undergone a slight reversal. As experienced as Clair was in the game of flirtation, successfully managing to keep at least three suitors on her bow, Corinne knew with certainty that this man Juan Martel would have no such dealings with her, and Clair would be heading for trouble if she attempted to encroach on their relationship.

Her brooding dark blue eyes rested on the cool tiles of the dining room floor on this thought. Clair had shied at marriage, as Juan had. There simply hadn't been a good enough offer for her to contemplate giving up her very full social life, but she had never met a man like Juan Martel, she thought ironically. Now that he owned the business that he had once been a partner in, he must surely be a very wealthy man. Her brooding eyes left the flooring and rested on the man opposite her, who appeared to be engrossed with his own thoughts as he stared down into the coffee cup he held in his lean strong fingers.

There was no doubt in Corinne's mind that once Clair had met Juan Martel she would think she had won the jackpot! Had the man been any other man than the sophisticated, experienced Juan Martel, Corinne would have found it in her heart to feel very sorry for him, for Clair would have gone in with guns blazing and an arsenal of feminine wiles to back her. She still would, Corinne thought dryly, only this time it would be Clair who had all Corinne's sympathy. It would be a battle that she would lose hands down.

Corinne pulled herself up at this thought. Now why should she be so certain of that? Clair had the looks, and goodness knows, all the tactics to ensure victory. Her glance rested on Juan Martel's strong jaw. He was human, wasn't he? Then why should she think that he would not accept the loaded bait Clair would be sure to throw his way?

As if her thoughts had reached through to Juan, he looked up at her suddenly and for a moment in time her questing dark blue eyes met his enigmatic grey ones, and she looked swiftly away. She had the answer; this man's heart would never rule his head. There would be no dalliance where he was concerned. She recalled his look of hauteur when reminding her that the marriage would be a business arrangement only. She knew with certainty that he had his own rules of conduct, and that Clair had fallen far short of his strict code.

Corinne took another sip of her coffee, and watched Juan finish his. Any moment now he would explain the terms of the will to her, she thought, as she shook her head in answer to his enquiry of whether she wanted a refill, and her eyes followed his tall figure as he walked over to the sideboard to replenish his cup.

He would play with Clair, she thought, reverting to her earlier musings, as a cat plays with a mouse, but that was as far as it would go. He would enjoy leading her on. She gave an involuntary shiver. He could be cruel, she was sure of that too. He had made no secret of the fact that he despised Clair for her mercenary attitude towards her grandfather, and the way she had not shown an interest in him until his imminent demise, so he would have no compassion where she was concerned.

At this point Corinne found herself hoping Clair would not get a flight out in time for the funeral. It was all very well to say that Clair deserved such treatment, she had hurt many men in much the same way, but Corinne did feel a certain responsibility towards her. When she got back, she decided, she would turn the charming and almost irresistible Juan Martel into a thoroughly disagreeable character— slightly balding, and stout to boot, thus quelling any interest Clair might show towards her unknown husband!

The sharp shrill sound of a bell broke off Corinne's musings, and she glanced towards Juan. 'The doorbell,' he explained dryly. 'Maria will see to it.'

A moment later Maria entered the dining room holding a cablegram in her hand which she gave to Corinne, and Corinne, wondering what Clair wanted to know now, because it must have come from Clair —no one else would contact her in Las Palmas— asked to be excused as she opened the envelope and read the contents.

After she had read the message, she blinked and re-read it again as if her eyes had deceived her, then with a hand that slightly shook she passed the cablegram over to Juan, receiving another shock by the way he barely glanced at it, as if he knew precisely what the message said.

It seemed to Corinne that time had stood still while she grappled with the bald fact that Clair had failed to get the necessary documents over to her in time. Her desperate-sounding 'Try and see if my verbal agreement is good enough for Mr Martel,' had come a little late, she thought bleakly. She then saw that Maria was still in the room, obviously waiting to see if there was an answer to the cablegram, and she shook her head at her. 'No reply,' she said, through stiff lips, and as soon as Maria had left she turned towards Juan Martel, bracing herself for the fury that she was sure would be released upon her now that they were alone.

CHAPTER FOUR

WHILE Corinne waited for the storm to break over her, she glanced at Juan Martel out of the corner of her eye, and saw that he did not look a bit put out. In fact, he had a bland look about him that made her wonder if he was suffering from the effects of shock and had temporarily lost his vocabulary.

She swallowed. It would be nice if he stayed that way until she was en route for home and safety, but she doubted if she was going to have that much luck.

As the silence around them lengthened Corinne, thinking someone ought to say something, began with, 'Apparently there's been a ghastly mistake made. I thought you had Clair's written authority, and you obviously thought that I had it,' she ended lamely, and swallowed again.

Juan did not reply, but continued to study her in that calm but watchful way of his, like a volcano about to erupt, she thought shakily. 'I suppose neither of you will inherit now,' she went on despondently, realising a little too late that she was hardly helping matters by bringing that up now.

'The terms of the will have been adequately fulfilled,' he replied quietly, breaking his silence at last,
but his eyes were still watchful as they met Corinne's
surprised ones.

'You mean it's all right?' Corinne exclaimed, feeling a surge of relief flow over her.

'I married a Clair Suter,' he replied carefully, 'that
was all that was required of me.' He gave an odd
cynical smile before adding softly, 'Gabriel would
have heartily endorsed my action.'

Corinne thought that this was an extremely odd
remark to make, but she was too relieved to work out
the significance of it. Clair was going to inherit her
grandfather's estate after all, and she and Joy would
be able to stay on at the cottage.

'How long will it take you to see to things your
end?' he shot out at her suddenly.

Corinne came out of her happy musings with a
puzzled frown, not quite getting the question; to report back to Clair, he meant, she thought, when she
had put her mind to the question. 'As soon as I can
get a flight,' she replied quickly. 'I suppose you'll
want to see Clair eventually, won't you?' she asked
happily.

'I ought to have said how long will you need to
make the arrangements to bring your child back
with you?' he said quietly, but very distinctly.

For the second time that morning, Corinne's world
rocked under her feet and she stared at Juan. 'I beg
your pardon?' she said in a faint voice. As she had
earlier doubted the evidence of her eyes, she now
doubted the evidence of her ears.

Juan gave her a small tight smile, and with studied

deliberation produced a form out of his inner jacket pocket and tapped an elegant forefinger on the form. 'This is the marriage certificate. You are now my wife. I see nothing unusual in requesting your presence at my home forthwith. I do understand that you will need time to make certain necessary arrangements before you can join me, and I'm hoping that there will be no hold-ups in the procedure,' he added, in what sounded like a warning note to the stunned Corinne.

'You can't hold me to the marriage,' she managed to whisper, when she had got her second breath. 'You know very well that I thought I was standing in for Clair.' Her eyes widened as a thought suddenly struck her, and she recalled that he had not answered her question on whether he had heard from Clair when they were on the way to the register office. 'You knew all the time that the authority hadn't come through, didn't you?' she accused him, in a voice of half-wonder as if she couldn't really believe it herself.

His calm nod, and casual, 'Of course,' sent a shiver of apprehension along Corinne's spine, and she was momentarily bereft of speech.

When she was able to answer, all she could say was, 'Why? Why should you do a thing like that? You don't know me. It's ridiculous!' She floundered here, still not able to accept what had happened. 'But you said that it would be a business arrangement,' she went on, desperately trying to make sense of it all.

'And so it will be,' he replied quietly. 'I do not intend to force my attentions on you, if that's what you're afraid of.'

'Then why must I stay at your home?' demanded

Corinne, feeling a little better now that they were back to the business side of things. 'Why can't I go back to my home? There's Joy, and——' she took a deep breath, and shook her head bewilderedly. 'I just don't understand any of this,' she said crossly.

'I'm simply offering you and your child a home,' he answered haughtily. 'It is normal for the husband to provide for his wife, isn't it?' he added harshly.

'In any other circumstances, yes,' bit back Corinne, determined to fight for her independence from this very forceful man. 'And Joy's my sister, not my child,' she tacked on indignantly, a light flush staining her alabaster cheeks. 'And you still haven't answered my question,' she flung at him. 'Why have you changed your mind?'

His steady appraising look went slowly over her, making her cheeks turn a deeper shade of pink. 'Because it suits me,' he replied casually. 'You're uncomplicated, pleasant to look at, and I'd say loyal to the point of stupidity.'

'Thank you,' murmured Corinne, in a low voice. She had asked for the last observation. Coming to Las Palmas in Clair's place had been stupid, more stupid than she had ever visualised.

'I am tired of the sophisticated woman,' he went on, as if discussing the weather. 'Gabriel was right—I ought to marry. There are times when a woman in the background can stabilise one's affairs.'

Corinne's eyes widened at this cool assertion. Easier and safer for him to play the field, she thought scathingly, and if he thought she was going to agree to become his shield for future skirmishes in the romantic line, he had better think again! 'I'm afraid you've chosen the wrong woman,' she replied, with a glint in her eye. 'I'm quite happy as I am. You were right when you said I was uncomplicated. I intend to stay that way—but thanks for the compliment,' she added hastily on seeing the flash of fury in Juans' eyes.

'You appear to be under the delusion that you have a choice,' Juan said harshly. 'You have no choice. If you refuse to comply with my wishes in this matter, Clair will inherit nothing. The cottage you seem so attached to will then have to be sold.'

His cold ultimatum reverberated around the shocked Corinne and she stared at him. 'But you can't do that!' she exclaimed. 'If Clair doesn't inherit, neither do you! I'm not that stupid!' she added furiously.

'I'm afraid you're wrong,' he said softly, reverting to the silky tone that Corinne so disliked. 'I fulfilled my obligations in the will by marrying you. All Gabriel was concerned with was keeping the business in the family, and I shall keep to my side of the bargain by seeing that this is done. It is up to you to see that Clair receives a share in the will.'

'But that's blackmail!' Corinne got out shakily, feeling in the middle of a nightmare.

'I would rather say rough justice!' he grated out. 'What did either of you care for an old man who longed to have his family around him? All his granddaughter wanted was his money. And you? You were motivated by the fact that you would lose your home. Were they good enough reasons, do you think, to hoodwink Gabriel on his deathbed? Well, both of you should now be satisfied. His granddaughter gets the money, and you will get a home—not, of course, the home you would prefer, but you will be

adequately provided for. I'd say the pair of you came
out remarkably well, wouldn't you?' he demanded
savagely.

Corinne closed her eyes. On the bare face of it,
all that he had said was true. But there was more to it
than that. She longed to scream out at him that she
hadn't envisaged herself arriving in time to participate
in a deathbed scene. Had there been time, she would
have told Gabriel Mowbray the truth, she had hated
that part of it. As for being afraid of losing her home,
there had been Joy to consider. It was essential for her
sister's health to remain in the country, but this hard
man wouldn't understand any of this, she thought
wearily.

She knew that she was beaten, but she couldn't give
up just like that. Surely Clair would have a say in the
matter? She voiced her thoughts. 'What makes you
think that Clair will accept these conditions?' she asked
through stiff lips. 'She's bound to feel responsible for
what's happened,' she added, hoping she had found a
flaw in his reasoning.

Juan gave a grim smile at this. 'You are backing a
loser, you know, if you are relying on Clair's conscience. I very much doubt if she has one, particularly if
it affects her expectations.'

Corinne looked quickly away from his mocking
eyes. He was right, of course; the only help she could
expect from Clair would be in packing her case for
her!

'I would not advise you to suggest that she con-
tests the will, either,' he added softly. 'It wouldn't
make good publicity for either of you, would it? I
suggest that you do precisely what I want you to do.
Go back, and make the arrangements to join me at

the earliest opportunity. I will provide you with enough money to cover your return flight with your sister. I would also suggest that you say nothing to Clair about this conversation. As far as she is concerned, her authorisation did not arrive in time, and she must be thankful that I was so strongly attracted to her envoy's charms that I married her.'

Corinne stared dully at the floor. As he had so coldly pointed out at the start, she had no choice but to do exactly as he wished. She closed her eyes. Why on earth had she to have the same name as her cousin? None of this could have come about if the family hadn't had an illustrious forebear of the name. She thought of his rather snide remark about her charms. He could hardly have said the same to Clair, she thought, but he hadn't seen Clair—a light suddenly appeared in the gloom around her. He wanted a wife—no, that was not right—he wanted someone in the background, and Clair would need no persuading to be that someone once she had met the handsome Juan! Her thoughts raced ahead. It couldn't matter to him which Clair Suter took on the role he had outlined to Corinne.

She looked up at Juan who was watching her every action, and, she surmised, enjoying her discomfiture, but she wasn't beaten yet. 'Look,' she said quietly, willing herself to sound calm and reasonable, 'you want a wife—well, someone in the background,' she amended hastily on seeing his autocratic brows shoot up, 'and so you married Clair Suter,' she continued, refusing to be put off by a warning look in his eye. 'Why don't you ask my cousin to fulfil that obligation for you? I know her well enough to be certain of a favourable reaction towards the idea.' She gave

him a small smile, but her eyes pleaded with him to
release her from the harsh contract he had made
with her.

'Because I married you,' was his implacable answer.

'You married a Clair Suter!' Corinne retorted
angrily. 'What does it matter which one fits the bill?'

'To me, a great deal,' he replied harshly, 'and in
case you're in any doubt you'd better take a good
look at this certificate.'

He thrust it at Corinne, then sat back and folded his
arms across his broad chest.

Corinne could not quite see the point of such an
exercise. She knew that a marriage had taken place,
she had been present, hadn't she? It was not until
she saw the names that had been filled in on the certificate that she realised the significance of his words.

That Juan Carrero Martel had married Clair
Corinne Suter there was no doubt whatsoever. There
was also no doubt whatsoever that Juan Martel had
been fully aware of what he was doing. Her name
leapt out at her, loudly proclaiming this bald fact,
for it had not been necessary to add her second Chris-
tian name. Clair's was Mariana, after her mother,
and Corinne could have supplied this had she been
asked to do so.

'You left nothing to chance, did you?' she said
bitterly. 'Supposing there was someone else? I might
be engaged to someone for all you know, but you
wouldn't even have considered that, would you?'
she added in a low voice.

'Are you?' His grey eyes held hers in a mesmeric
hold, and Corinne was forced to tell the truth.

'No, as it happens I'm not, but I might have been,'
she insisted stubbornly.

'It was a logical conclusion that you weren't,' he replied dryly. 'You were worried about not having a roof over your head, weren't you? This would hardly have been the case had there been a man to watch over you. Now enough of this prevarication. How long will you need to settle things your end?'

Corinne licked her dry lips and tried to think coherently, finally giving it up with a sigh of exasperation. 'How do I know?' she replied dazedly. 'You calmly throw all this at me and expect me to answer a question like that. I need time to think,' she went on steadily, making herself remain calm. 'You do realise what this means to me, don't you?' she demanded. 'It means leaving my home, and uprooting not only me but Joy as well.' She gave him a pleading look. 'I'm not sure that I can go through with it.' She pressed her trembling lips together and willed herself not to break down. 'I know what I— what we did, was wrong, and if I'd had a chance I would have told Clair's grandfather the truth and why Clair couldn't come.'

She faltered here on seeing his firm lips twist in a cynical sneer. He did not believe her, she could see that he didn't, but she made herself go on. She was fighting for her freedom. 'Surely just the knowledge that you're married will be sufficient for your needs,' she went on doggedly. 'If you require my presence at any time, I could put in an appearance, couldn't I?' she suggested hopefully.

'Out of the question,' Juan snapped back at her, hardly allowing her to finish the sentence. 'As you so rightly pointed out earlier, I leave nothing to chance. I did not plan to have a wife living the other side of the world from me. When I said that I needed someone in the background, I meant the immediate background, living in my home. A wife's place is with her husband.' He gave Corinne a mocking smile. 'You'll get used to the idea,' he told her grandly. 'Remember that I am allowing you to bring your sister back with you. I could have insisted that you came alone.'

Corinne gasped. Of all the hateful, autocratic creatures! 'There is no question of my leaving her,' she replied stiffly. 'She's still at school.'

Juan's dark winged brows lifted at this, and he gave Corinne a hard searching look as if trying to determine whether she was telling the truth. 'And there are only the two of you?' he queried.

Corinne gave an abrupt nod. 'We lost our parents years ago,' she replied in a low voice. 'Our grand-parents brought us up, now there's only Joy and I.'

He stared down at his well shaped hand lying along the arm of his chair, and Corinne felt a surge of hope flow through her. Would he now release her from the impossible position that he had manoeuvred her into?

'And Joy is how old?' he asked, after a moment's silence.

'Fifteen,' said Corinne, her eyes searching his enigmatic grey ones for some sign of hope. 'She's another six months' schooling to do, and several examinations to sit,' she added meaningly.

'We have some exceptionally good schools here,' he replied quietly, instantly quelling the hope that Corinne had began to nurse. 'If they are not suitable, then I shall get her a private tutor,' he added haughtily. 'You will have no cause to worry over your sister.'

No cause to worry, thought Corinne, now on the verge of hysteria and praying that it was all a bad dream, and that she would soon wake up to normality. One thing was certain, she told herself grimly, if it was a dream, wild horses wouldn't drag her to the register office the following day!

Her apprehensive glance went towards Juan Martel and she saw that he was glancing at the expensive-looking gold watch on his wrist. 'I have booked you a seat on the one-thirty flight,' he said casually. 'I shall give you ten days in which to settle your affairs and provide you with the return tickets so that there will be no hold-up your end.'

Stunned, Corinne looked at her watch. It was just after midday.

'You have ample time in which to pack and catch that flight,' Juan told her bluntly. 'I shall now take you back to the hotel, and then out to the airport.'

CHAPTER FIVE

CORINNE did not remember much more about the rest of that morning. She knew that Juan had taken her back to the hotel, and had paid her bill while she had packed her cases.

At no time had she been in charge of anything, and his forceful attendance stopped short only at the airport barrier, and even then Corinne saw that he did not leave the airport until the plane taxied down the runway prior to take-off, and away out into the blue horizon towards the shores of England.

During the flight, Corinne had four hours in which to come to terms with the devastating fact that she had married a man she did not know—a marriage that she had undertaken in the mistaken belief that she was participating in the ceremony on Clair's behalf. Only the hard cold feel of the gold ring that lay in her jacket pocket where she had slipped it after the service told her that what had happened was no dream, but cold reality.

According to custom, she knew that she ought now to wear the ring, but she baulked at the very idea, as if by leaving it where it was, out of sight, she could somehow avert the inevitable.

During these pulsating thoughts, it did occur to her that Juan Martel and Gabriel Mowbray had more in common with one another than just a business partnership. Gabriel Mowbray had sought to dominate his family to the point of suffocation, hence the reason for Clair's mother's flight from home all those years ago, and her refusal to place herself and her daughter back into the same trap that she had managed to escape from. Juan Martel had the same ruthless, dominating outlook, and as Corinne was now his wife, she was going to find out with a vengeance what it was like being married to such a man.

As the miles slipped by, she found it harder, not easier, to come to terms with her predicament. Every mile passed brought her nearer to home and the inevitable barrage of questions that she would have to face from Clair, not to mention the outspoken Joy, who knew her a little too well to be fobbed off with less than the truth.

There were, she reasoned silently with herself, two ways in which she could handle the bizarre situation. One would be to flash the ring in front of Clair and say something on the lines of : 'Oh, by the way, Juan knew you wouldn't be able to get the authorisation over in time, but we married anyway, seeing that I had the same name, and it was a case of love at first sight !'

Corinne closed her eyes. She would never get away with that, she thought miserably, and that left the second and more probable explanation—the truth ! She could tell Clair how she had come to find herself married to a stranger, and she had better put on her thinking cap, or contact that legal wizard of hers and do something about it !

Corinne looked out at the great expanse of sky around the plane winging its way across the fluffy white clouds that looked like puffs of cotton wool against a canopy of brilliant blue. For a brief span in time she was lost in the beauty of the heavens. The threat of the future, as outlined by Juan Martel, should she fail to comply with his orders, had no place in this world of timelessness.

The feeling of certainty that in the end all would come well did not unfortunately last long, and soon Corinne was back to her worries.

It was all very well asking Clair to extricate her from the mess that she had inadvertently landed herself in, but how willing would Clair be to help her when she was faced with Juan Martel's ultimatum ? If Corinne refused to go back to Las Palmas, Clair would not inherit a penny, and knowing Clair, Corinne knew that she would contest the will. She also knew what the result of such a move would be. Men like Juan Martel did not bluff. He had meant what he had said about exposing their money-grubbing efforts to gain access to Gabriel Mowbray's money. Corinne gave a shudder; it didn't bear thinking about.

To take her mind off these disturbing thoughts, her glance strayed to the middle-aged woman seated next to her, who was having a cosy chat with a friend who sat across the narrow passageway alongside her. Both women were well tanned, Corinne noticed, and had had an enjoyable holiday. Every now and again something that they had said would be endorsed by one of the two equally tanned elderly men who sat in the seats directly behind Corinne, and who were obviously the women's husbands. 'I wonder how long Ted will go this time before getting that cough of his back,' commented the woman seated next to Corinne. 'Do you know, Ivy, I don't remember him having to ease up once during the holiday. Those coughing fits of his take a lot out of him, you know.'

'Too busy enjoying himself!' came the jocular answer from one of the two men at the back. 'That's right, isn't it, Ted?'

Laughter followed this observation, but the woman next to Corinne was not going to be put off. 'No, honestly, Ted. You said yourself that the climate suited you, didn't you?' she appealed earnestly to her husband.

Corinne did not listen to the said Ted's reply, she was too busy with her own thoughts. Would the Canarian climate help Joy's trouble? she wondered. If it would, then it would be worth all the change and uprooting that was in store for them. Even worth leaving the cottage, she thought sadly, and her eyes were wistful as she thought of the home that she and Joy had been so happy in for the past two years.

When Clair had first suggested that Corinne and Joy should move into the cottage that she had just bought situated on the edge of a small Kentish village, Corinne had had doubts on the wisdom of such a move. From what Clair had told her of the cottage, and its partly isolated position on the fringe of the village, it had sounded ideal, for Corinne was not one for social gatherings, and had valued her privacy. While she had listened to Clair as she had enthused about the merits of having somewhere to go, away from the crowded London scene, Corinne had thought it sounded a little too good to be true, and decided to withhold her judgment until she had seen the cottage, even though the need to get some good country air into Joy's lungs was a pressing matter. The trouble was that she knew that Clair was apt to make snap decisions and then change her mind with equal rapidity.

With this thought well in mind, Corinne had gone to look at the cottage, and found herself hoping that it would not come up to expectations, and that she could honestly say so, and therefore refuse Clair's offer.

One look at the small cottage tucked away behind a thick hawthorn hedge, had settled the matter once and for all for Corinne, for she had fallen in love with it. As she went through the small but compact rooms, with their low oak beams, she fervently hoped that Clair would not change her mind this time.

Later, when she had wandered through the small village, she had seen an advert for a part-time bookkeeper required by a local market gardener, in the window of the small post office, and had made a note

of the telephone number given for the applicants to
ring. She could still recall the sense of wonder she
had felt on seeing that advertisement, and she had
known she would get that job. It had been that sort of
day for her, when all was right, everything had had
a magical touch about it. You could not argue with
these signs that shouted at you to go ahead, and
Corinne certainly did not, but accepted the offerings
of fate with a grateful heart.

Employment had been another factor in her earlier
worries. Would she be able to get the type of work
she had been trained for? Her natural aptitude for
figure work at school had led to her taking a course
in bookkeeping in her final year, and although she
had not known it at the time, this training had stood
her in good stead when she had had to take on the
task of looking after Joy when their grandparents
died. This had meant finding some employment that
would enable her to work from home, and bookkeeping was the ideal answer. There had been several
small firms around the district that they lived in that
could not afford to employ a full-time bookkeeper,
and after placing an advertisement in a local food
store, Corinne soon found herself gainfully employed
at home.

Two weeks later, she and Joy moved into Hawthorn Cottage, and Corinne, having successfully applied for the job at the market garden only a short
distance away from the village, settled down to
country life.

She moved restlessly in her seat on the plane. She
might have known it was too good to last, she
thought sadly, and wondered miserably what the
future held for her. She sighed. Clair wasn't going to

like it one little bit. It would mean finding someone
else to caretake for her, although she should not have
too much difficulty in finding a replacement, she
thought sadly, as she could not see anyone passing up
the chance of living in such delightful surroundings.

It was seven-thirty when the taxi Corinne had
hired to take her from the sleepy railway station
to the cottage drew up in front of the cottage. For the
first time since she had lived there, Corinne felt no
pleasure as she gazed towards the diamond-shaped
glass window panes of the sitting room that looked
out on the short drive, the curtains of which were
drawn cosily against the dark of the evening, and a
warm orange glow of light shone out invitingly into
the still chilly atmosphere.

As Corinne paid off the taxi and gathered her cases
up she expected to hear the front door open with its
customary slight squeak and to find herself receiving
a hug from the no doubt relieved Joy, on her early
return from foreign parts.

When no such welcome was afforded her, and she
had to search for her key to let herself in to the cottage, she knew Joy was not at home, and this fact
worried her until she recalled what evening it was,
then she relaxed. Joy would be at the local youth
club with her friend Jean.

Leaving her cases in the tiny hall, Corinne took a
deep breath and prepared herself to meet Clair and
face the somewhat embarrassing questions that
would inevitably crop up. For the life of her she
could not see how she was going to handle the explanation of how she had come to find herself married
to Juan Martel—not only married, but forced to ac-

cept his ultimatum to return to Las Palmas in ten days' time.

Well, here goes, she thought miserably as she walked towards the sitting-room and on opening the door, was assailed by the loud wailing of a police siren emitting from the film on the television that Clair was apparently engrossed in.

Her amazed, 'Good gracious! I didn't hear you come! Oh, switch that thing off! I was only watching to help pass the time.'

Corinne took her time in carrying out this small chore, and Clair asked impatiently, 'Well?' in a voice that showed her tension. 'Is it all right? Did he accept my verbal agreement?'

Corinne nodded abruptly, and sat down, suddenly feeling very tired. 'Yes, it's all right,' she said quietly. 'You will inherit a half share of your grandfather's estate. Juan Martel inherits the other half.'

Clair's arms were flung into the air in a gesture of pure exhilaration. 'Blast this ankle,' she said impatiently. 'I want to rush out and celebrate, and here I am stuck in this position,' she grumbled. 'Well, we'll celebrate anyway! A large vodka and lime for me,' she said happily, and gave the wan-looking Corinne a hard stare. 'You look peaky, I should have a brandy if I were you,' she advised Corinne cheerfully, and Corinne was obliged to produce the celebratory drink.

While she poured out their drinks, Corinne's mind was busy working out how to get over the next hurdle, and she poured herself a liberal dose of brandy thinking she might well need some kind of stimulant. So would Clair, she thought grimly, if she knew the whole truth.

She was in the act of handing Clair her drink when it occurred to her that she was not going to tell her the whole truth. She would follow Juan Martel's advice—well, nearly, she told herself, since she could not see herself repeating his veiled suggestion that he had succumbed to her charms, Clair was not likely to believe that for one moment. She would just have to think up another more plausible explanation.

'Cheers!' called the exhilarated Clair, and took a sip of her drink. 'You know what this means, Corinne?' she went on, her blue eyes narrowed in speculation. 'I'm rich—really rich! Bill Harding, that's the legal eagle at the office, has a friend working in Las Palmas, and he got him to put a few feelers out about Grandfather's affairs. According to Bill, he had the Midas touch in all his business dealings, and was disgustingly rich.' She placed the rim of her glass against her carmined lips. 'And Mother didn't let on,' she said, with a shake of her blonde head. 'To think that she walked away from all that!'

Corinne eyed her dispassionately, and surmised that the said Bill Harding had been acting under Clair's orders in surveying her future prospects. It was highly unlikely that he would carry out such a task of his own volition. As for Clair's mother walking out on a fortune, there were some things money couldn't buy, and one day Clair might find that out for herself, she thought ironically.

'How do you fancy giving up that petty little job of yours and running an eight-bedroomed manor for me?' Clair suddenly asked the startled Corinne, and went on before Corinne had got her breath back. 'We've outgrown this poky place,' she said, her eyes flicking disdainfully over the small cosy sitting-room they sat in.

Corinne stared back at Clair in dismay, the thought that she was going to sell the cottage taking prior attention above all else. 'Oh, Clair, you're not going to sell the cottage?' she exclaimed in a horrified voice.

'Of course I am!' Clair snapped back crossly. 'I can afford a much better place than this. I know just the place, too,' she went on smoothly. 'The manor house here. It's that huge place on the hill opposite the church, you must have seen it. They're distant relations of Ralph Patterson's, you know, and he was only telling me the other day that they were putting it on the market, said something about them not being able to afford the running costs.'

Clair went on happily about how lucky she had been in hearing about the proposed sale, and how she would now be in time to stop the house going on to the open market, but Corinne was no longer listening to her. She was too busy pondering on the cruel vagaries of fate. To think that she had been put through twenty-four hours of anxiety and shock, only to learn that it had all been in vain. Even while realising that there was very little chance of her managing to extricate herself from the bonds Juan Martel had placed around her, she had still sub-consciously clung to a ray of hope that all would come right in time, and that she would be able to settle down again with Joy in the home that they both loved so much.

That Clair was now expecting them to uproot themselves and live in a huge mausoleum, for that was exactly what Corinne thought of the large house on the hill that overlooked the village, was really

the last straw, and she wanted to shake Clair hard
for adding to her misery.

'With all that room,' Clair went on in a dreamy
voice, unaware of the furious thoughts going through
Corinne's mind, 'we shall be able to put my friends
up for the weekend. We'll have a house-warming
party first, of course. I shall have to make a list out
of who I want to invite. You can ask a few people
too, if there's anyone you'd like to invite,' she told
Corinne magnanimously.

'I'm afraid you'll have to count me out,' Corinne
got in swiftly, unable to bear even the thought of the
swinging, noisy parties that Clair was so addicted to,
of which there would be many in the not too distant
future.

Clair's finely plucked eyebrows raised at this
adamant statement of Corinne's. 'You're tired,' she
said after a moment's thought. 'It's all that travelling. We'll talk about it tomorrow,' she added soothingly.

'Tomorrow won't make any difference!' said
Corinne irritably. 'Juan Martel offered me a job, and
I accepted,' she added swiftly, surprising herself with
the calmness of the statement. 'We'll be leaving for
Las Palmas on the twenty-fourth of this month—Joy
and I, that is.'

Clair's eyebrows shot up even higher, and Corinne
saw the familiar pout of annoyance on her lips. 'Just
like that?' she exclaimed furiously. 'Leaving me
when I'm practically helpless! Well, it's out of the
question! Who else can I rely upon to see that every-
things done the way I want it done?' she demanded
querulously. 'You'll just have to tell him you can't
take the job, whatever it is. And what about Joy's

schooling? The whole idea's ridiculous!'

'There are some good schools in the Canaries,'
replied Corinne firmly, again surprising herself.
She had never thought to find herself on the same
side as Juan Martel! 'Mr Martel said that he was
sure we could find a suitable one for Joy,' she added
quietly.

'You did get chummy with him, didn't you?' Clair
remarked, studying Corinne through narrowed eyes.
'Tell me, what's he like? It's odd to think that
he's my husband, and I don't even know what he looks
like. He wouldn't be tall, dark and handsome, by any
chance, would he?' She gave a high titter of amusement.
'No, that would be too much to ask, wouldn't it? I see
him as a stout balding character—I mean, he can't be all
that much to write home about if he's a bachelor, can
he? I must say his letter to me sounded a bit disapprov-
ing.'

Corinne looked quickly away from Clair and studied
the glass in her hand. Her mind's eye showed another
similar scene, where Juan Martel's strong lean hand
held his glass of whisky. She knew she ought to tell Clair
the truth, but she couldn't resist getting her own back
on the autocratic Juan Martel. 'Oh, I'd say your sum-
ming up was pretty accurate,' she replied casually, hoping that Clair would not spot the spark of unholy
amusement lingering at the back of her dark blue eyes.
'And by the way, he's not your husband, he's mine!'

The amusement was now in danger of getting out of
hand, and Corinne wasn't too sure that it wasn't
hysteria, for she badly wanted to laugh at the amazed
expression on Clair's face. 'Are you having me on?' she
demanded furiously, then as a thought occurred to her
she visibly blanched. 'You told me that I couldn't

couldn't inherit unless I married that man. If you've messed things up, you'd better go to the Canaries!' she added viciously.

Corinne swallowed the impulse to laugh. If she gave way to this desire she knew she would never stop. It was hysteria, of course, and she recognised it as such. She had been put through a variety of emotions during the past twenty-four hours, and this was nature's way of releasing the tension that had built up inside her.

She swallowed again, and forced herself to remain calm. 'I didn't mess anything up!' she said, managing to inject a note of indignation into her voice. 'You did! You were certain you'd be able to get the authorisation over in time, and you didn't! In the end there was a bit of a mix-up,' she went on quickly, not giving herself time to dwell on the true facts of the matter. 'I thought Juan Martel had the necessary papers, and he thought I had them, and we didn't discover this until after the wedding when I got that cablegram from you telling me that there'd been a hold-up.'

Corinne fell silent for a few seconds. The next part could be tricky, she thought, but she had to go on. 'I was dreadfully worried then, and thought that you wouldn't inherit, but Mr Martel said that as I had the same name as you had, it would be all right. The terms of the will stated only that he should marry Clair Suter—and he had done that.' She looked away from Clair. 'He had my passport, you see,' she went on slowly. 'I suppose he had to give it in to the registrar, and the marriage certificate has my name on it, that is to say, my full name, Clair Corinne Suter, and not yours.' She let this fact sink in to the

fully attentive Clair, before adding, 'Well, when I
saw that certificate, I could see what had happened
—so could Mr Martel,' she gave a light shrug. 'Of
course, he felt he was partially responsible for the
mix-up, and rather feels responsible now for me,'
she swallowed quickly. 'He wanted to know all about
me, and I told him about Joy—then he offered me
a job out there—in one of his businesses. There's
nothing else to it,' she added firmly. 'It's a business
transaction, if you like, and the marriage will be
anulled as soon as possible.' She hesitated before
adding, 'It seemed too good an opportunity to pass
up. I mean, actually living in a place like that with a
job thrown in. The climate will suit Joy too, I heard
someone on the plane say how much better her husband was, and he'd got some kind of chest trouble,'
she tacked on, now almost babbling in her anxiety to
prove that all was well.

To her vast relief, Clair did not seek verification on
any of the points raised. If she had, Corinne would
have been lost, and would have had to tell her the
plain unvarnished truth of how she had come to find
herself trapped into marrying the forceful Juan Martel !

In the event, Corinne found that she need not have
worried. Clair was too relieved herself on the vital
point that she would inherit a fortune to seek further
enlightenment, and it occurred to Corinne that Juan
Martel had not been far off the mark when he had
intimated that she would get no help from Clair
when faced with the possibility of losing out on the
inheritance.

Now that she was assured of a rosy future, Clair
turned her attention back to Corinne. 'It might not

only be a job he's offering you,' she said meaningly. 'Have you thought of that?'

Corinne's cheeks turned pink at the very thought of Juan Martel turning amorous. 'There's absolutely no chance of him taking advantage of the situation,' she replied firmly. That at least was the truth, she thought ironically. 'Don't worry about that side of things. I'm not. I'm looking forward to Joy and me getting a sun tan!'

'While I have to struggle through at this end,' Clair replied complainingly. 'I don't see why you couldn't have put him off a few months—you might have thought about me,' she added crossly.

'You'll be having that plaster off next week, won't you?' asked Corinne lightly, feeling that she could relax now that she had got through the worst hurdles. 'And you can now afford to throw your job up, can't you? You won't have any trouble in getting a housekeeper, you know. There aren't that many jobs going in the village. You'll have them lining up to be interviewed. You'll love every minute of it!' she added accusingly.

Clair pouted, but it was plain to see that she was starting to relish her forthcoming position as the village benefactor. 'I still think you'll have to watch it,' she remarked meaningly, not ready yet to relinquish her complaint where Corinne was concerned. 'He might find Joy's presence slightly de trop!'

'Who's de trop?' queried Joy as she entered the sitting-room, and giving Corinne a hasty hug, settled herself on the arm of her chair.

Corinne gave Clair a warning look before she replied hastily, 'Not you, dear,' and went on quickly to change the subject. 'I wasn't able to bring you anything back in the souvenir line, but when you've heard my news I don't think you'll be disappointed.'

Joy gave her an odd appraising look, then looked at Clair. 'Everything's all right, isn't it?' she asked in a doubtful voice.

Clair gave a slight moue at this. 'Oh, fine,' she replied in a sarcastic voice. 'Corinne's got landed with a husband in the Canaries, that's all!'

'Clair!' expostulated Corinne, giving her a glare. 'You know very well what happened! You ought to be grateful to me for not kicking up a fuss about it. If I had, you might not have inherited, have you thought of that?' she demanded furiously.

Clair's pencilled eyebrows rose laconically. 'If you say so,' she retorted sulkily, 'although I'm sure it could have been handled a better way. This Juan Martel doesn't sound very bright to me,' she added meaningly.

Corinne took a deep breath and tore her gaze away from the stupefied Joy, whose wide eyes said more than words. If only Clair knew that her observation was the last accusation one could level at Juan Martel. 'I do say so,' she answered, forcing herself to remain calm. 'But if you're going to be awkward about it, then I shall simply back out of everything, but don't blame me if you lose out on the inheritance. It won't look too good for you, will it, if everything comes out?' she stated quietly.

It was plain to see that Clair had not ever envisaged such a happening, and now that she thought about it, she was not at all keen on the idea. 'I was only thinking of you,' she said, hastily backtracking on her previous outlook. 'And that I shall miss you,' she added plaintively. 'I suppose I was really only thinking of myself. You must accept his offer. I would have done if I'd been you,' she added placatingly, and gave a feigned resigned sigh. 'I'm only glad for your sake that he's stout and balding, and not the type to push his luck,' she tacked on, a little spitefully to Corinne's way of thinking. She then gave an exaggerated shrug. 'Oh, I know you won't have anything to worry about in that direction,' she ended piously.

'Will someone please tell me what's going on!' demanded Joy, who looked about to explode.

'Go and put her in the picture, Corinne,' said Clair, with a touch of exasperation. 'I've some phone calls to make.'

Corinne was only too pleased to comply with this autocratic dismissal of Clair's. 'Come on, Joy, let's go to my room,' she said, her voice sounding as relieved as she felt. Clair would not put up any more opposition to their going to the Canaries.

Joy had said nothing while they had gone up the stairs and seemed to be lost in her own thoughts, but hardly had the bedroom door closed behind them than she rounded on Corinne with, 'What exactly did she mean by my being de trop?' she demanded.

Corinne looked away from her indignant eyes and wondered how to explain this very uncalled-for remark of Clair's. 'Well, it's just a phrase that——' was as far as Joy allowed her to get.

'I know what it means!' she said indignantly. 'I want to know why she said it. And why you married someone you don't really know, if you did!' she ended unbelievingly.

Corinne patiently explained the circumstances that had led up to the wedding, giving Joy the same version that she had given Clair. It sounded better that way. 'And so when he offered me the chance of a job out there—well, I accepted it. I mean, we'd never get the chance of going to such a place for a holiday, would we?' she appealed to the now incredulous-looking Joy. 'We can look on it as a long holiday, can't we?' she went on hastily. 'And if we don't like it out there, I suppose Clair will always take us back,' she ended lamely, wishing she could believe in what she was saying, for she was almost certain that Juan Martel had no intention of releasing her from her obligation, regardless of whether they were happy or not.

'This Juan Martel,' began Joy, favouring Corinne with a searching look. 'Is he as dumb as Clair thought?' she asked the now wary Corinne.

Corinne shook her head, making the waves of hair curl close to her small heart-shaped face and emphasising her attractiveness to her young sister's knowing eyes. 'No, he isn't,' she replied firmly. 'It's a business arrangement, and really we ought to be grateful to him. He's offered us a home as well.'

'Oh, dear,' Joy sighed, 'now I know what Clair meant by my being de trop! What if he knew what he was doing?' she asked.

'I'm not quite sure what you're getting at,' lied Corinne stoutly.

'Of course, you wouldn't be!' replied Joy, in the manner of an adult speaking to a child. 'You're too trusting, that's your trouble. It would have been easy for him to work things his way, though, wouldn't it? Suppose he took a fancy to you?' she demanded. 'If he's out to ravish you, you'll spend most of the time dodging his pudgy advances. Have you thought of that?' she asked the astounded Corinne, who was wondering just who was the elder of the two of them!

'Where,' she asked when she had got her breath back, 'did you get such a ridiculous idea from? Ravish indeed! Have you been reading some Victorian novels?' she demanded.

Joy tried hard to look indignant, but her sense of humour let her down and she gave a little chuckle. 'Not Victorian,' she replied airily, 'some of Jean's romances. She gets them from the library. According to most of them, you haven't lived unless you've had to fight for your honour!'

Corinne's dark blue eyes opened wide at this. 'You don't believe everything you read, do you?' she asked in a reproving tone.

'Of course not!' replied Joy loftily. 'All the same,' she added meaningly, 'just let him try it on, that's all! It's as well I'm going with you. I'll look after you if he gets any amorous ideas where you're concerned!' she declared with a glint in her grey eyes.

Corinne blinked at this firm assertion, and it occurred to her that in future she would have to keep a wary eye on her young sister's reading matter, although she had to admit to herself that once Joy had met the handsome Juan Martel, all she had read in the romantic line would inevitably cause her to have second thoughts on the matter. But it was not like that at all, Corinne thought bleakly, and Joy would be in for a big let-down before many days had passed.

CHAPTER SIX

TEN days later Corinne and Joy were on their way to Las Palmas—Corinne with an assurance from Clair that if things got tough, and it didn't need much imagination on Corinne's part to know what she was referring to, they would always be welcome at the Manor.

During the short interlude between their packing and making the necessary arrangements for the journey, Clair had constantly referred to her new home as 'The Manor', in spite of the fact that the actual name of the property was Larkfield Hall, and Joy for one was heartily sick of the subject.

'I'm not sorry we're going,' she confided to Corinne a few days before their departure. 'You'd be run off your feet with all those parties she's planning on giving.'

These sentiments were heartily endorsed by Corinne, and it took the edge off her anxiety for their future welfare. As the time had drawn nearer for their departure, she had constantly reminded herself what life would have been like for her and Joy if it had not been for Juan Martel's ultimatum. It was quite plain to her that they would have eventually had to make the move away from Clair and her grandiose schemes for the future, if she didn't want to find herself completely embroiled in the dual role of housekeeper and social secretary, a job she would have hated, and as for Joy, there was no doubt in

Corinne's mind that when she left school in six months' time, her services would also be called upon, in one capacity or another, and that was something Corinne would not stand for, not to mention Joy's thoughts on the matter!

As the plane winged its way through the blue skies, and towards their destination, Corinne glanced at Joy whose eyes had scarcely left the small round window beside her, and Corinne could sense her pent-up excitement with the flight. It was a completely new experience for her, as it had been for Corinne during her first flight to Las Palmas, but most of Corinne's earlier travels had been taken in a state of anxiety, and she had not had the time to savour any pleasure from the journey. Coming back had been worse than going, she recalled, as she remembered her stunned feelings at that time.

Her lovely dark blue eyes softened as they rested on Joy's animated features as she gazed out of the plane window, afraid to look away in case she missed anything. Whatever the future held, she told herself, she was grateful for the chance of giving Joy this pleasure, and somehow she would try and see things through. Whatever position Juan Martel had in mind for her, it could not be worse than the one Clair would have pushed her into. One thing she did know, and that was that Joy's fears of spending her time dodging Juan Martel's advances would soon sink into oblivion. As to how Joy would react to the forceful Juan's autocratic way of going about things, she couldn't even hazard a guess. The only man in her life from her babyhood had been her grandfather, who had been a mild-tempered man, and who had always found time for his granddaughters, even though he must at times have been very tired.

She watched as Joy slipped off her school raincoat, still keeping her eyes on the panorama around her, and once again took pride in her younger sister's flair for dressmaking as her eyes fell on the blue and white polka-dot dress she wore, one that she had made herself.

With not a great deal of money to spend on clothes, this natural flair of Joy's to make or renovate dresses had been a blessing for Corinne, and Joy had had the added advantage of being able to watch her grandmother, who carried on a small dressmaking business at home, at work during her growing-up years. When it was realised that Joy had inherited her grandmother's skill with the needle, her grandmother had encouraged her to use this skill by passing on some of the work for her to do, while supervising every step of the way.

Corinne had wanted her to eventually go to college to study dressmaking, for although she had a natural aptitude for fashion, jobs were not all that easy to come by unless you had qualifications. Given that chance, Corinne was certain that Joy could become a top designer. She had no ambitions for herself, but where Joy was concerned, she had many. She sighed. What would happen to those ambitions now?

Approximately four hours later the plane touched down at Las Palmas' small but busy airport. Corinne had been instructed to let Juan Martel know their departure time from London Airport, and having done so, she was certain he would be waiting for them at the airport.

For Joy's sake she had managed to maintain an outwardly calm composure during the flight, but as her eyes skimmed over the small knot of people waiting in the airport lounge to greet the new arrivals, her pulse rate soared to a tattoo when she encountered the cold grey eyes of the man standing a little apart from the others. The man who was now her husband, and whom she knew nothing about, apart from the fact that he knew what he wanted out of life, and went singlemindedly after his goal, regardless of the cost to others.

Joy, ignorant of the fact that her new brother-in-law was now striding towards them, said, 'Which one is it?' as her glance rested on two elderly balding men waiting near the door of the reception lounge.

Corinne was saved the necessity of replying as Juan, covering the short distance between them in his long lazy stride, was holding a lean tanned hand out towards the amazed Joy. 'So you're Joy,' he said in that deep well-modulated voice of his. 'Welcome to Las Palmas, and your new home.' He then turned his sardonic gaze on to the apprehensive Corinne. 'I trust you had a good flight out?' he queried politely.

'Yes, thank you,' replied Corinne, slightly surprised at the calmness of her voice, and wondering if she ought to introduce Juan to Joy, as her new brother-in-law, but she was given no opportunity as Juan requested that she show him which were their suitcases.

'I suppose he was too busy to meet us,' whispered Joy to Corinne, as they watched Juan collect the cases indicated by Corinne. 'Still, he sent a nice reception committee, didn't he?' she added appreciatively, as Juan signalled a porter to take the luggage out of the airport and stow it in his car parked in front of the reception lounge.

Joy gave another show of appreciation at the sight of the gleaming Mercedes, and gave Corinne a nudge. 'I think I'm going to like Las Palmas!' she murmured in a low voice, after Juan had settled them in the back of the car, then closed the trunk and tipped the porter, and got in the car.

Corinne was given no time to have a private word with Joy to warn her against making any references to her 'podgy' husband in Juan's hearing, and sat in agonised suspense as the car swept out of the airport precincts and towards their destination.

Corinne's first impression of Gran Canaria had been a disappointing one once they had left the airport behind, for the scenery was bare and deserted-looking, not unlike desert country with patchy scrub land that would barely provide a living for those who worked on the land, and was hardly in keeping with the tourist image of the Fortunate Islands.

Now, as she watched Joy's eager gaze as she stared out at the passing scenery, she wondered if her impressions were the same. She did know that the island was short of water, and had had to import it, for there had been a notice up in her hotel bathroom requesting frugal use of the water, politely requesting that a shower would be more economical than a bath. It appeared that even here in the isles of eternal sunshine, climatic change had brought about a period of drought, in spite of the fact that the Isles enjoyed spasmodic rainfall throughout the year.

The journey to Las Palmas took forty minutes, and if it seemed a long time to Corinne on her previous visit, it seemed even longer on her return.

Juan gave them a summary on the Islands' history, and how they had been conquered by the Spanish in a long-drawn-out war that had begun five centuries ago, and had taken half a century to end. Corinne suspected that this commentary was given purely for Joy's benefit, and knowing that Joy had done her own research on the Islands' past, was vaguely amused by her rapt attention to Juan's remarks.

It was when Joy began to ask Juan a few personal questions that Corinne began to feel apprehensive again. Her innocent, 'Have you always lived here?' question made Corinne dart her a quick frowning look in the hope of dissuading her from following this very personal line of conversation. However, the question had now been asked.

'My forebears took part in the conquest,' he replied, with a hint of pride in his voice.

Far from being discouraged, Joy then asked quickly, 'Do you work for Mr Martel?' for which she received a sharp dig in the ribs and a warning look from Corinne, who wished she could somehow become invisible.

Juan's grey eyes sought Corinne's in the driving mirror above him, and Corinne was obliged to say hastily, 'I didn't have time to introduce you. This *is* Mr Martel, Joy.'

There was a long pregnant silence as Joy digested this information, and she stared accusingly at Corinne. The look plainly said, 'Bald and podgy, indeed!'

'It is, in fact, Señor Martel,' Juan supplied in a dry tone. 'But you will call me Juan. Your sister is now Señora Martel,' he added significantly, and Corinne's eyes fell quickly to her hands now twisted together in her lap.

Corinne felt rather than saw Joy's swift glance at

her before she said in a voice that showed that she still
hadn't recovered from the shock that she had received,
'I suppose I'm Señorita, then?'

Juan's white teeth flashed against his deep tan. 'Or
Miss Suter. It will be as you wish,' he replied, showing
that Joy's reaction had pleased him.

To Corinne's relief, Joy subsided into a thoughtful
silence after this, but every now and again she would
cast a surreptitious look at Corinne, who was well aware
of the trend that her thoughts had now taken, thanks to
the romances read by kind permission of her friend
Jean! She also knew that she was in for a big let-down
when she found that Corinne had told the truth when
she had said that the marriage was a business arrangement.

Now they were entering a built-up section, and
Corinne breathed a sigh of relief, for she knew that they
were on the outskirts of Las Palmas and would soon arrive at their destination, wherever that was.

Juan's deep voice then broke into the sisters'
silent musings. 'We are now coming into Las Palmas,'
he commented, as he skilfully negotiated the power-
ful car through the maze of traffic they had joined,
then looked at Corinne through the car mirror again.
'Your hotel was in this section,' he commented,
'though it's not the most popular area for the tourists,
they appear to prefer to be nearer the centre of the
town. They can always get a taxi down to the beach
if they want a day's sunbathing. The taxis, as you
probably noticed, are remarkably cheap compared to
other places.'

Corinne preferred this type of conversation to the
previous one that had looked like getting a little out
of hand. 'I thought the hotel was in a good position,'

she said quietly. 'It looked out on to the sea-front, and there seemed to be a lot of guests.'

'It's just a case of preference,' Juan replied. 'It depends on what sort of holiday you want. There are many such hotels along that particular stretch of beach, but they mainly cater for tourism only. By that, I mean half board—a buffet breakfast and dinner in the evening. It works out cheaper than full board, of course.'

'And your hotel?' asked Corinne, determined to keep this innocuous conversation going, but was unable to stop a sardonic note from entering her voice.

She saw him glance swiftly at her again before he answered abruptly, 'You get what you pay for,' and Corinne had a distinct feeling that this reference included more than the hotel business. 'We are known for our service and cuisine,' he went on haughtily. 'We could be classed with Claridges of London. There is only one Martella.'

Corinne's deep blue eyes widened at this. 'Is that the name of your hotel?' she asked, then added pithily, 'I rather thought it might be Mowbray and Martel—or something like that,' she tacked on waspishly, thinking that the name was hardly in keeping with Gabriel Mowbray's wishes.

'It has always been Martella,' Juan replied haughtily. 'The hotel has been the family business for over a century. I think perhaps you are referring to the business Gabriel and I were partners in. That is an entirely different project, and need not concern you.'

Corinne looked away hastily, feeling a flush stain her pale cheeks and Joy's eyes upon her. She felt as if he had slapped her in front of Joy, and she hated him for it. If there was anything good in that cold rebuke of his, it was that Joy could no longer be under any illusion as to their relationship, and this would surely make things easier for Corinne in the future.

The car then glided off the main highway and entered a long curving drive bordered with flowering shrubs, and then as the car swept around a bend, a huge rambling mansion-type house came into full view, built, Corinne presumed, in the Spanish style, for there were numerous balconies with trailing vines and flowers that would provide a breathtaking outward view of the old building during the summer season. It was hard to conceive that although the temperature never went below fifty, this was the island's winter period.

In the well-tended gardens surrounding the hotel were Grecian-style statuettes, placed in the centre of what would be, later, a magnificent show of tropical flowers enhancing the view. Corinne could well imagine how the scene would look at night, for lighting arrangements had been provided to highlight the whole area. She drew in her breath sharply. As Juan Martel had so bluntly pointed out, you get what you pay for, and she wondered why he had bothered to interest himself in another business when it was obvious that the Hotel Martella was doing so well.

The amount of activity centred on the wide parking area in front of the hotel proved beyond doubt that however astronomical the charges were, there was no shortage of patronage, for private cars and taxis were moving in a constant stream either arriving at or leaving the hotel.

'Welcome to Martella,' said Juan, as he negotiated the car past the impressive front and what appeared to be a circuit round the hotel to the back of the premises where several cars were parked in a cemented space provided, Corinne presumed, for guests and staff. Juan guided the car to a stop in a space well clear of the other cars, and what was obviously his personal area, as it was only a few steps away from the back entrance to the hotel.

Corinne was still smarting from Juan's unnecessary earlier rebuke and when they got out of the car she barely glanced at him, and stood beside Joy as he retrieved their cases from the trunk and then ushered them into the hotel. 'I shall leave the introductions until later,' he commented, 'and take you to your rooms first.'

On hearing this, Corinne visibly brightened, for it sounded as if she and Joy would be given rooms next to each other and, she hoped, well away from this hateful man's proximity. As the marriage was a business arrangement, this was how it should be she thought, and felt a sudden lift of her earlier depression; it looked as if things might turn out well, after all.

They entered into a plush-carpeted corridor and walked through to what looked like a small reception area. It was, in fact, the inner sanctum of the large reception lobby where only the staff had access, for directly in front of them was the long horseshoe-shaped reception desk with several uniformed clerks attending to the incoming and outgoing flow of guests.

Juan was just ushering them towards an elevator on the right of the reception area when a clerk, who had been about to take a key down from the board at the back of him, caught sight of them. 'Señor Martel!' he called, with a hint of urgency in his voice.

Whatever he had wanted Juan to see to was never explained, as Juan waved a dismissing hand towards him. 'Later, Alonso!' he commanded haughtily, and it was significant that the clerk simply nodded his head and did not attempt to argue, but carried on with his work.

Corinne, getting into the elevator with Joy, watched Juan's long lean forefinger press the required button on the panel and had a shrewd suspicion that nothing short of a fire in the hotel would distract this man from his purpose. The thought was not a comfortable one, and for once she wished that Joy would say something— anything—for she had been remarkably quiet for once, too quiet for Corinne's liking.

If Juan sensed anything unusual in his new wife and her young sister's silence, he did not attempt to break it, but seemed content to leave them to their musings. Corinne felt as if she had applied for a job, and having been successful, had been allowed to bring her sister with her. If things continued in this way, she would be more than satisfied, she told herself firmly. The bare fact that the job had not been advertised, and if it had been she would not have applied for it, but had been pressganged into accepting it, she refused to dwell on!

The elevator stopped on the third floor and Juan escorted them down a corridor that branched off from the public section of the hotel, at the end of which was a door that clearly displayed the word 'Privada' in large gold lettering. As Juan opened the door and ushered the girls in, Corinne felt a sense of keen disappointment. So much for her hopes of Joy and her being allotted rooms out of the proximity of the autocratic owner of the hotel !

From what Corinne had seen of the interior of the hotel with its discreet aura of wealth, it seemed almost commonplace against the surroundings she now found herself in. On the rich embossed papered walls of the corridor they were walking through hung portraits in large golden frames that looked of great antiquity. The corridor widened a little further on, and soon they came to a spacious hall, its proportions made even larger by two large mirrors set in the wall on either side of the glass-panelled doors.

Preceded by Joy, Corinne then found herself ushered into what she presumed was the lounge, and as her bemused gaze rested on the rich tapestries and fine furnishings around her, she found time to wonder once again why Juan Martel had sought success in other business enterprises. This room alone spoke of wealth and success, and not recently acquired either, but of years of plenty.

It would appear that she had slightly misjudged his financial position, not to mention the reason why he had been so determined to comply with Gabriel Mowbray's terms as stated in the will, even to the extent of burdening himself with a woman he did not know, let alone love.

She glanced back at Joy standing in the middle of the room, with her shoes sinking into the thick luxurious carpet and looking much as Corinne herself felt, absolutely lost, as if they had perhaps wandered off the tracks somewhere and would soon be summoned back to reality.

There was simply no answer to Juan's smooth, 'I hope it is to your liking,' remark as he showed them over the rest of the suite, that comprised a study, dining room, four bedrooms, two bathrooms and a room that could have been used as a dressing room, or could have been used as a fifth bedroom.

They were shown into all the rooms except one that Corinne presumed was Juan's room, and the apprehension that had been growing steadily within Corinne and had increased in volume at each room they visited was considerably lessened when they reached the last two rooms at the end of the corridor and Juan placed the cases down, signifying that these were their rooms.

As they entered the rooms, Corinne saw that they were of equal size and of equal splendour, except that one had a blue decor and the other primrose yellow. The smaller of the two bathrooms was adjacent to the rooms, and this would alleviate any waiting for the bath. Corinne was so relieved that she actually forgot her earlier annoyance with Juan, and commented on the rooms in a favourable manner.

With this initial welcoming tour over, Juan glanced at his watch and remarked, 'It is almost four o'clock,' and favoured first Joy and then Corinne with what Corinne thought was a patronising smile. 'I expect you could both do with some refreshment. I shall have your tea sent up to you in the lounge.' He gave a slight frown. 'I must now go and see what little problem Alonso has on hand that requires my urgent attention. If business permits I shall join you later,' and with that he left them.

There was a short stupefied silence immediately after his departure, then Joy, who had appeared to have lost her voice for longer than Corinne could ever remember, suddenly found it. 'Bald and podgy!' she gasped, as she collapsed on to the comfortable-looking single divan with a satin bedspread. 'I just don't believe it!' she continued in a wondering voice. 'Pinch me, Corinne, or else I'll think I'm dreaming!'

She was silent for a second, then gave a low chuckle. 'Poor Clair,' she said, and looked at Corinne. 'She'll never forgive you,' she added happily, and swept her arms in an embracing gesture around the room. 'All this and heaven too!' she quoted with a mischievous glint in her eye.

'I don't see where the "heaven" bit comes into it,' Corinne replied irritably. 'And if you mean what I think you mean, I'm here to work, remember?' She gave the amused-looking Joy a stern look. 'You might find yourself doing the washing-up, but I don't suppose that's occurred to you, has it?' she asked ironically.

Another chuckle greeted this warning. 'Can you see that lord of the manor allowing his sister-in-law to work in the kitchen? I can't,' Joy said dryly.

Corinne cast her a reproving look. 'I suppose that's what they called the heroes in those books, is it?' she queried caustically. 'Well, the sooner you realise that life isn't like that at all, the better,' she added firmly.

Joy shot her a wicked look. 'Well, he does qualify for the hero role, doesn't he? I think he's beautiful,' she said dreamily.

Corinne raised her eyes to the ceiling in hopeless resignation. 'Shall we freshen up?' she said brusquely. 'I could do with a cup of tea.'

The mention of refreshment broke Joy's reverie and she scrambled off the bed announcing that she was starving and hoped that there would be adequate eats sent up.

After a quick wash and tidy-up, they made their
way back to the lounge. Corinne hoping that whatever the said Alonso's problem was, it would keep
Juan occupied for quite some time and allow her
and Joy to become accustomed to their opulent surroundings, although she suspected that it wasn't only
their surroundings that had made Joy tongue-tied
for such a long period, but had more to do with the
overbearing but undeniably handsome Juan Martel.

This aspect of the situation had never occurred to
Corinne, but Joy was at an impressionable age. She
was also a very sensible girl, Corinne reminded herself, and if she was about to develop what was known
as a crush on Juan Martel, she had no doubt that it
would be of a short duration, particularly if he made
Corinne unhappy.

On their entry into the lounge, a tall slim, well-
dressed woman got up out of the chair she had been
occupying and held out a white, slim, heavily ringed
hand in welcome to them. 'I'm Carmen Martel,' she
introduced herself, 'and I presume you're the reason
Juan demanded my presence forthwith.' Her welcoming smile was open and frank, and was echoed in her
light brown eyes.

As she took the proffered hand held out to her,
Corinne reciprocated with, 'I'm Corinne Suter, and
this is my sister Joy,' which would have been fine,
had it not been for the fact that she was now Corinne
Martel, but she had no time in which to correct herself as Juan suddenly appeared on the scene.

'Ah, Carmen!' he exclaimed with a note of
pleasure in his voice, and then looked at Corinne.
'I take it you have introduced yourselves?' he asked.

Corinne gave a swift nod, wondering what relation-

ship this pleasant-faced woman had with Juan. She was
not old enough to be his mother, and yet not young
enough to be his sister—his brother's wife, perhaps? If
he had a brother, that was, and she felt a spurt of annoyance that she should know so little about the man
she had inadvertently married.

'Well, Carmen, what do you think of my wife?' he
said abruptly, and then carried on as if he had just announced the evening menu. 'I hope you will take her
under your wing. Joy, as well, of course. We shall have
to find a suitable school for her in due course, although
for six months it seems hardly worth it,' he added
thoughtfully.

Corinne's embarrassed eyes went swiftly to the thick
carpet under her feet. She had not given the poor
woman a chance, she thought, as she perceived the look
of shock Juan's bald announcement produced, although she recovered swiftly enough to reply in a slightly bemused tone. 'We hadn't actually got that far with
the introductions. You did say your wife, didn't you?'
she demanded.

Corinne felt Juan's eyes upon her and felt compelled
to look up at him. 'I would have explained,' she said
lamely, 'but you came in.'

Juan nodded thoughtfully, and smiled at Carmen
Martel. 'Well, let's begin again, shall we? This,
Carmen, is my wife, Clair, whom I persuaded to marry
me—against her better judgement, I might add. And
this young lady is Joy Suter, her sister.' His steely
eye fell again on Corinne. 'Clair, this is Carmen Martel, my step-mamma, although she won't thank me
for introducing her as such,' he added, his mood
changing to one of amusement as he looked at Carmen.

If Carmen had been confused before, she was doubly so now, and her expression said so as she looked at Corinne and said, 'Corinne or Clair?'

'Corinne,' Joy got in swiftly. 'We already have a Clair in the family,' and her tone of voice said plainly that one Clair was enough!

'Corinne, please, I would prefer it,' Corinne interjected quickly, not liking the way Juan's fastidious eyebrows had lifted at Joy's intervention.

'I prefer Clair,' he said in a soft, no-nonsense voice, and this time it was Joy's eyebrows that rose and Corinne had a feeling that Joy was not quite so enamoured with her new brother-in-law at that moment.

A throaty chuckle suddenly erupted from Carmen Martel. 'It looks as though you're in for a rebellion, Captain,' she said delightedly. 'I think I'm going to get on with my new in-laws! And I prefer Corinne to Clair. Clair sounds a little stuffy, doesn't it?' she queried with amusement.

Juan was not amused, and his eyes had remained on Corinne while Carmen was stating her preference, and Corinne knew that he expected her to abide by his wishes in this, but she did not feel inclined to do so. Up until now this autocratic man had made the rules—rules she had had to follow regardless of her own feelings in the matter. He had trapped her into marriage purely on a whim of his to provide a stabilising effect on his affairs—at least, that was the way he had put it, but Corinne would have put another interpretation on it, one that was a little nearer the truth. Not content with this, he now wished to change her name to one that she had little liking for, and she had no doubt that given the time he would mould her very character into pliant acceptance of his plans for her future.

This thought frightened her and gave her the courage to meet his eyes and reply to his unspoken command. 'Well, that's easily settled,' she said, forcing a light note into her voice, 'you will call me Clair, but I see no reason why anybody else should.' She saw the swift flash of fury this stand of hers brought to his cold eyes, but she was determined to show him that there was a limit to what could be expected of her. 'I don't promise to answer to the name of Clair,' she added bravely, 'seeing that I don't regard it as my name, but I'll do my best.'

Juan's haughty look plainly said that her best was simply not good enough. 'Yet the name served a useful purpose, didn't it?' he queried silkily, and at Corinne's swift flush he gave a grim nod. 'There is time enough to accustom each other to our likes and dislikes,' he added significantly, and to Corinne's relief then directed their attention to the tea tray that had just been brought in by a member of staff, and the conversation turned to lighter matters.

Had it not been for the presence of Carmen Martel, Corinne could not have imagined how she would have got through that period of acute embarrassment. She was not exactly looking forward to the time when she and Joy would be alone again, for Joy could not have missed Juan's swift change of attitude towards her when she had attempted to thwart his wishes.

It was as well that she should be acquainted with the true facts of the matter, and Corinne had hated having to gloss over the truth, but she did not see what else she could have done; there were times when a white lie was preferable to the bald truth, and this had been one of them.

These disquietening thoughts were soon dispelled by Carmen's obvious interest in the sisters. She asked innumerable questions about their background, and was genuinely interested in the subject of village life.

In her turn she told them that she had been brought up in Mexico, but her family had moved to Gran Canaria when she was eighteen, and she was ashamed to say that that was the limit of her travels, but she had been so happy in her adopted home that she had not had the urge to travel.

It was here that Juan intercepted with an amused, 'Nonsense! you could not bear to leave the business!' and this produced another throaty chuckle from Carmen who did not attempt to refute the statement.

This was the only intervention from Juan, and Corinne, who had been aware of his cold eyes settling upon her when she least expected it, fervently wished that his presence was required elsewhere, and when the telephone rang and was answered by him, her wish was granted almost on cue, and she could have shouted with relief when she heard him say that he would be right down.

It seemed to Corinne that once he had left them the atmosphere changed from an intimidating one to a freer and considerably happier one.

Carmen could not have missed Corinne's evident relief at Juan's departure from the scene, but she made no comment and turned her attention to Joy. 'I like that dress,' she said. 'Would you think me very rude if I asked you to stand up and turn around so I could see the back?' she asked.

Joy's brows went up at this strange request, but she did as she was asked.

Carmen stared at the dress through slightly narrowed eyes. 'I could do with five dozen of that pattern,' she stated, to the amazement of Joy and Corinne, and then grinned at their astonishment. 'I own a boutique,' she explained, 'and I'm always on the lookout for new ideas. I particularly like the extra flounce that's been added to that three-quarter sleeve, it's chic without being fussy,' she declared. 'Did you get it in a large store or a small boutique?' she demanded.

Joy gave a look of amusement at this, and Corinne said proudly, 'Neither! It's all her own work!'

Carmen blinked. 'You mean you made it up from a pattern?' she asked.

Joy shook her head. 'I design all my clothes,' she replied quietly. 'When we can't afford to buy the material, I renovate our old ones.' This was said without a trace of boastfulness.

Astonished, Carmen looked at Corinne as if seeking confirmation, and Corinne supplied it by saying quickly, 'It's true. You see, our grandmother was a dressmaker, and Joy's taken after her. She's very good too,' she added proudly.

'I can see that,' replied Carmen with an animated look in her eye, then she clapped her hands together in a manner that suggested that she had had an idea that pleased her very much. 'Didn't Juan say that you had only six months' schooling to do?' she asked Joy suddenly.

Joy gave a puzzled nod at this and glanced at Corinne.

'If we'd been in England,' Corinne replied, 'she would have gone to college when her schooling was over.' She hesitated here, not quite knowing how to

put the bald fact that she doubted if the same facilities existed in the Canaries, and ended lamely with,
'We shall have to see about that, of course, later.'

'Why not let her take up the work straight away?'
demanded Carmen. 'I see no reason why she should
not.' She shrugged her broad shoulders. 'What is
six months anyway? It is only really time to prepare
oneself for one's career.' She shrugged again. 'College
is only necessary to gain the required certificates,
and then the tramp round the fashion houses to gain
employment.' She gave Joy a hard earnest look. 'Here,
it is work that counts far more than certificates.
Come and work for me, Joy. I have all the facilities
that are required. You can design away to your
heart's content. I shall pay you a salary, of course,
I am not asking for your services for nothing. Well,
what do you say?' she demanded of the amazed Joy.

Joy looked as if she had just been bequeathed her
dearest wish, as indeed she had, and her eyes held a
mixture of hope and pleading as she looked at
Corinne. 'Can I?' she asked her, in a hushed voice
holding her breath for the answer.

Corinne blinked hard. She felt as if she needed time
to assimilate all that had happened in such a brief
span of time. She was married to a man she did not
know, and now her young sister was being offered a
job—and what a job! doing the very work she had
set her heart on, and Corinne had set her hopes on
her obtaining at some future date.

For a moment she found it hard to say anything,
and that moment must have seemed like hours to the
waiting Joy, not to mention the anxious-looking Carmen, who, unable to bear the suspense, said quickly,
'I can assure you the hours will not be too tedious
—no more really than if she were at college, and I

shall keep a strict eye on her for you.'

In the end all Corinne could do was to give a swift nod of assent, and was then engulfed by a jubilant Joy hugging her and saying 'Thank you!'

At this point Juan walked in on them, and Carmen explained the reason for the excitement. 'Meet Estillo's new designer,' she said happily. 'I have just engaged your sister-in-law's services.'

Juan's expressive eyebrows shot up at this, and he looked at the flushed and sparkling Joy. 'So is that what you want?' he asked her, to Corinne's annoyance, who felt that it was none of his business, but Joy did not see it that way. 'Oh, yes!' she breathed ecstatically.

Juan's eyes left Joy and rested on Corinne. 'And it pleases you?' he asked her haughtily.

Corinne was able to answer that. 'Very much,' she replied with a certain amount of reserve in her voice; she had not forgotten his insistence on calling her Clair. 'All we want now is a job for me,' she went on steadily, as it had suddenly occurred to her that with Joy away all day she would be entirely alone and the prospect looked grim. 'I suppose you don't happen to require a bookkeeper, do you?' she asked the now apprehensive-looking Carmen, whose eyes were on Juan.

'I'm afraid there is no possibility whatsoever of your filling such a vacancy, should one occur,' Juan said harshly before Carmen could reply.

The indignant answer Corinne was about to give Juan on this dictatorial statement of his was forestalled by Carmen hastily asking Joy when she would like to start work. The question was meant to distract Corinne from embarking upon another disagreement with Juan, and although Corinne recognised it as such, there was nothing she could do about it, though her furious eyes spoke volumes as she stared back at him.

Joy's equally hasty answer of, 'As soon as you like,' made Corinne wonder whose side she was on!

'I think you ought to allow them a few weeks in which to get settled in first, Carmen,' Juan replied firmly, determined, it seemed to the seething Corinne, to stamp his authority on everything. 'As yet they have seen nothing of their new home. I intend to show them around,' he added haughtily.

The 'few weeks' remark made Joy cast Carmen an anxious look, and Corinne knew that she was afraid that she would withdraw her offer of employment in the face of Juan's reluctance on the matter.

Carmen, however, soon dispelled this fear by giving Juan a rueful look. 'Of course, Juan,' she replied soothingly. 'I was so eager to engage Joy's help that I forgot everything else.' She looked at Joy. 'When Juan takes you to the Catalina market, do look at the caftans there. Some are of pure silk, and it will give you an idea of the kind of materials we have to work with.'

The sparkle of anticipation was back in Joy's eyes as she nodded happily at this direction.

This ought to have put Corinne into a better mood, but she was still seething over Juan's autocratic ruling as far as she was concerned, and she wished Carmen would whisk Joy off with her there and then, and give her the chance of a word in private with this autocratic, overbearing male whom it had been her misfortune to not only meet, but inadvertently marry!

CHAPTER SEVEN

THE silent wish of Corinne's to have a word with Juan was not realised until much later that day, after Carmen had gone, and Joy had gone to bed a little earlier than her normal time, exhausted with the journey and the excitement of the day's happenings.

Carmen had departed shortly after they had had tea, and she had promised to visit them again a day or so later, but this time making it an evening visit, to be certain of finding them in.

During dinner that evening, taken in the dining room of Juan's private suite, most of the conversation had been carried on by Joy and Juan. Joy traitorously showed an almost pathetic wish to please Juan, making Corinne wish that her foot was a little nearer to hers so that she could stem her enthusiasm for the proposed sightseeing tours with a nudge of her shoe.

As nine o'clock approached Joy, who had been trying unsuccessfully to keep her eyes fully open, finally gave up the struggle and with an apologetic smile at Juan asked if he minded if she went to bed. Having gained his amused reply that if she didn't, they would have to wake her to go to bed, she then glanced at Corinne, uncertain whether to go on ahead or to wait for Corinne to join her, but in his usual autocratic way, Juan had told her that Corinne would join her later.

In spite of the fact that Corinne had wanted a private word with him, she resented his high-handed

manner towards her, as if she had no will of her own,
and her resentment heightened at the casual way Joy
had accepted his stipulation and just gave Corinne a
crooked grin as she left the room—not caring one
whit, Corinne thought crossly, about leaving her one
and only sister in the clutches of this detestable man.
She could gain little comfort from the fact that whatever she had previously read in the romantic line, it
had obviously not influenced her; if it had, it might
just have occurred to her that her sister might be
spending the rest of the evening fighting for her
honour!

When Corinne came out of these hypothetical musings, she found Juan's eyes upon her, and to her vast
annoyance she felt herself flushing under his hard gaze.
'I think it as well if we had a little talk,' he said slowly
with an underlying hint of steel in his voice. 'Naturally,
you do not know a great deal about Spanish customs—
or how a Spaniard expects his wife to behave. I realise it
is different in England, and for that reason only shall I
grant you a little leeway in your behaviour. However, I
will and do demand absolute obedience to my wishes,
no matter whether it concerns your social or personal
pursuits. Our future association will be a much
smoother one if you abide by these rules, but if you continue to oppose me, you will make life extremely uncomfortable for not only yourself, but for Joy as well. I
could, for instance, ask Carmen to look elsewhere for
help.'

Corinne, who up until now had stared back at him
with a mutinous light in her eyes, now opened them
wide in disbelief. 'Surely you wouldn't—' she began.

'Oh, but I would!' he replied softly, before she

could finish the sentence. 'So you see it is entirely up to you. I shall not,' he went on grimly, 'expect to have to cover up another lapse such as the one that occurred this afternoon with Carmen. You are now Señora Martel, and in the eyes of the world you are my wife, and will be introduced as such. It will be necessary on certain occasions for you to play the role I have assigned you with a little more feeling than you have so far shown where the affections are concerned. I shall not expect any outward demonstrations, of course, but I shall expect absolute obedience from you. I will not tolerate any further exhibitions of outrage from you either, particularly when in company—is that understood?' he shot out at her harshly.

Corinne's wide eyes stared back at him. She was still reeling from his threat to ruin Joy's chances of an early start to her career, and found it hard to believe that he would go as far as that simply because Joy's elder sister had a mind of her own. What about Carmen? Would she agree to drop Joy at her autocratic stepson's instigation? Corinne's soft lips clamped together. She was sure that Carmen too had a mind of her own, and was not likely to change it; she had been too pleased with her success on recruiting Joy. 'Understood, but certainly not agreed upon,' she replied stiffly, finding it difficult to control her voice, she was so angry. 'As far as Joy's concerned, I doubt if Carmen will oblige you. She did not strike me as the kind of person who would back out of a proposition. Where I'm concerned,' she went on steadily, 'as I said before, you've chosen the wrong woman. You should have married my cousin. She would have loved being ordered around as if she was

a slave—it would have been a new experience for
her. It's always been the other way around, you see,'
she added dryly. 'I'm the opposite. Normally, I'm a
placid person. I hate scenes, or displays of emotion of
any kind. So far I have complied with your orders,
and providing what you ask of me is what I consider
reasonable, I shall continue to comply, but I see no
reason why I shouldn't seek some form of suitable
employment like Joy.'

She took a deep breath as she noted the warning
signals in his eyes, but continued steadily, 'I've seen
that you're a busy man, and surely you wouldn't
want me to sit around all day doing nothing. You
did say we ought to find out what our likes and dislikes were, didn't you?' she asked in what she hoped
was a reasonable voice. 'Well, I should dislike that
very much!' she ended firmly.

'Now I shall tell you my dislikes!' Juan replied
harshly. 'I abhor career women, and most certainly
do not intend to allow my wife to become one, so you
can put that out of your mind for a start. As for sitting around all day, there are calls you will be expected to make when the news of my marriage is
circulated around the island.' He gave her a haughty
look. 'Surely there is some pleasurable pursuit you
would like to take up?' He gave a nonchalant shrug.
'Something in the art line, perhaps?—or tennis?
You will have entrée to a number of clubs that cater
for such pursuits. Your daytime activities I shall not
interfere with, providing you act with decorum and
never forget that in the eyes of the world you are
my wife. Before very long you will know that you
have married a Spaniard, and will adapt yourself to
the Spanish way of life.'

He surveyed her flushed cheeks and fuming eyes. 'If you had understood this from the beginning, you would have known that Carmen would not go against my wishes. In her eyes I am the head of the family, a family that you now belong to, for better or for worse. The sooner you realise this, the smoother our relationship will be. I shall not,' he continued haughtily, 'make many demands upon you, apart from what I have already outlined.' He then glanced at his watch. 'I suggest now that you go to bed. It has been a long day for you, and you must be tired.'

Corinne had no intention of being dismissed as if she was a servant. She would go when she had settled this issue once and for all. 'I don't see much chance of a smooth relationship under those conditions,' she got out furiously. 'What about my wishes?' she demanded. 'I wasn't brought up to be a drone, and that's what you're asking me to become, isn't it? What right have you to make such demands on me?' she asked bitterly.

'The right of a husband,' he replied harshly. 'And you seem to forget that there are other rights I could insist upon if I were so inclined.' He gave her a slow appraisal, and Corinne's cheeks took on a deeper hue as she caught his meaning.

'I wouldn't advise you to try,' she ground out, hating him for playing with her, for that was what he was doing. If she had been a younger person, no doubt this threat would have worked, and would have sent her scuttling for safety. As it was, she knew very well that he was not in the least interested in her feminine charms in spite of that mocking look in his eye that pretended otherwise.

'That is another of my dislikes,' he said softly.

'Women who throw out challenges and who have no idea of what may be the consequences if accepted. It's an old gambit that I would normally simply ignore, but this is different, isn't it? You are challenging my authority, and that I will have to do something about.'

. He gave a grim nod at Corinne's wide and now apprehensive eyes. 'You have no cause to worry at the moment. I said that our association will be a business one and I shall not break my word. There are other ways to achieve your co-operation. Your sister's future, for example. With Carmen's help she will rise to the top of her profession, what Carmen calls a boutique is in fact a salon, and one that is patronised by the wealthy. The boutique side of the business is only a small diversion of hers and of no importance. Make no mistake, though, I shall not hesitate to advise Carmen to seek help elsewhere should you prove uncooperative. I am sure that after you have given this some thought you will see that there is no point in defying my orders.' He looked again at his watch and frowned in disapproval. 'It is time for my last rounds of the day,' he said curtly, 'so if you will excuse me,' and he walked to the door.

'Don't let me detain you,' Corinne got out through clenched teeth. 'I'd hate to spoil your routine!'

Juan paused as he reached the door and turned back to face her. 'What a wifely observation that was,' he commented tauntingly, 'and don't worry, you won't!' Then he left her.

Corinne glared at the closed door, then abruptly turned and made her way to her bedroom. He had been right when he had said that she was tired, but that was the only thing he had been right about, she thought furiously as she prepared herself for bed.

To her dismay, sleep did not come easily to her that night. She kept going over Juan's ultimatum in her mind, trying to find some way out of what looked like being a wretched future, for her anyway, if not for Joy. Juan had gambled on her putting Joy's happiness before her own, and in this he had been right, and Corinne knew it, but she wished desperately that there was some way that she could assert herself and live the way she wanted to live and not be beholden to such a man as Juan Martel.

The following morning Juan took Corinne and Joy on their first sightseeing tour; Joy, in excited anticipation of a day's outing, and Corinne wondering balefully if he could spare the time!

The first port of call was the Catalia Market that Carmen had mentioned, which was within walking distance of the hotel.

With the morning sun warming their shoulders as they joined the throng of tourists wandering around the stalls seeking out bargains to take home as presents, Corinne found her mood lightening. The warmth of the sun and the brilliant blue sky above them gave her no choice but to thrust her troubles away from her, pushing them into the background for later perusal.

The market area formed a large square that branched off from a line of shops that also catered for the tourists. These included several cafés that traded outside the premises on sectioned-off portions of space where the customers could enjoy whatever beverage they required while taking a breathing space from shopping.

Gay parasols over white-painted tables and chairs

gave the area a continental air that was delightfully
unfamiliar to Corinne and Joy. Each café had its own
individual colour scheme, and further along the row
was one that had an open-ended glass-covered roof
presumably to protect its patrons from the weather,
although the rainfall, normally adequate for the
island's needs, was scanty by English standards,
Corinne had learned from her study of the island's
history.

The stalls, though numerous, were set apart from
each other, and there was ample room to walk from
one to the other, noting the various goods for sale
and the different prices asked for the same article.

It was the dress stalls that Joy made a beeline for,
remembering Carmen's advice about the materials
available, and she would ask Juan the cost of the
various articles of clothing on sale and Juan patiently
obliged by transforming pesetas into pounds. While
these negotiations were going on, Corinne would
stand a little away from them feeling embarrassed
by Joy's intense concentration on the subject of price.
Corinne knew her well enough to know that she was
only seeking to establish the true cost of the finished
article offered for sale from the dressmaker's angle,
but to an outsider it could be interpreted as someone seeking a bargain and wondering if she could
afford it.

The caftans that Carmen had mentioned were well
displayed on the next stall visited, and when Corinne
heard Juan translate the cost into pounds, she visibly
shuddered and wished they could move on quickly
to the leather stall a few yards away. She had thought
that some of the dresses on sale had been expensive
by home standards, but the price of the caftans was

extremely high. Admittedly they were beautiful, some with gold thread worked in intricate designs around the high collars and on the full flowing sleeves. The sheen on the one Joy was now examining looked like silk, and very probably was, Corinne thought as she slipped away from the absorbed Joy and made her way to the leather stall, unable to bear the thought that by now Juan must have come to the conclusion that Joy was angling for a present, and might very well oblige, and that would not only embarrass Corinne but Joy as well, who had no such intention in mind.

Corinne was fascinated by the leather work— belts, intricately worked in Eastern designs, wallets, purses, sandals—all proclaimed the Eastern influence left by the Moors many centuries ago. Corinne took a deep breath of appreciation as her eye caught a tall, magnificent-looking African woman, wearing a turban and flowing robes, regally sweeping her way through the crowded section of the market. She then glanced back towards where she had left Joy and Juan and saw that they were about to join her. She took a deep breath of dismay when she saw that Joy was holding a large white carrier bag in her hand, and knew her worst fears had been realised— Juan had bought something for Joy.

Her grey eyes held an accusation in them as they met Joy's slightly embarrassed ones that told her that she had tried to prevent Juan from buying the gift but had failed.

It was here that someone hailed Juan and a young man strode forward towards them, giving the girls a hard scrutiny as he did so. 'I hear we're to expect another guest tomorrow evening,' he said, when he joined them, 'or perhaps two guests,' he added, giving the sisters an acknowledging nod of welcome.

Juan's reaction to this intrusion could not be called enthusiastic, Corinne noted, as he introduced them to the man. 'This is Miguel Blanco, an old family friend of ours,' he said, with a note of austerity in his voice. 'Miguel, this is Clair, my wife, and her sister Joy.'

While Corinne shook the hand Miguel Blanco held out to her, she noticed that the man was not as young as she had first thought. In his early thirties, she thought, as she murmured the conventional greeting in response to his rather effusive one, and decidedly did not like the way his dark eyes openly admired her, yet she sensed that there was more than just a passing interest in the meeting, and this was confirmed shortly afterwards by a fleeting remark of his to Juan, that Dolores would be charmed to meet his wife.

Corinne presumed 'Dolores' to be the man's wife, but she was startled at the thunderous look Juan gave Miguel at the mention of the name, and the thin cynical smile given by Miguel in reply to the look, and could then only assume that the unknown Dolores was one of the sophisticated women who no longer held any attraction for the man Corinne had married. She wondered caustically if her days were going to be enlivened by such meetings, all anxious to meet the woman who had succeeded where others had failed. How surprised they would be if they knew the truth, she thought ironically, and wondered about Carmen, and what she thought about the sudden marriage of her fastidious stepson.

When Miguel turned his attention to Joy, Corinne noticed with some amusement that Joy did not appreciate his bold scrutiny either.

Miguel Blanco, as his name suggested, was also Spanish, but cast in a different mould from Juan. He was not as tall as Juan for a start, and was inclined to plumpness as against Juan's lean but physically fit figure. His clothes, like Juan's, were casual, but because of his rounded proportions they did not fit snugly to his figure. Apart from these small diversions, he was what might be termed as good-looking in a showy way.

Eventually Miguel left them, after extracting a promise from Juan that he would attend the party being given the following evening, to which he had referred earlier, then favouring the girls with an embracing smile.

After his departure Juan's mood improved, and they continued the tour. Corinne's mood, however, had reverted back to a depressed one, and she wondered just what she had let herself in for when she had allowed Juan to dominate her very existence, although 'allowed' was hardly the right word. Blackmailed would be more appropriate, she thought miserably.

As it was then close on lunch time, Juan suggested that they take some light refeshment at one of the market cafés. This pleased both the girls, for it meant that they could sit and watch the passing throng that not only consisted of tourists but of people of many nations.

Las Palmas, Juan told them, was the largest city in the Canaries, and not only a city but a vital seaport as well, that held berths for all seagoing nations for commercial trading.

Juan order coffee and sandwiches for the girls,

but only had a glass of wine for himself, for although midday was the normal lunch time for the English, the Spanish custom was to take it much later, usually around three o'clock. The shops, Juan told them, had adopted the Spanish times of opening for business at nine o'clock and closing for lunch at one, a lunch that included a siesta and did not open again until four or five o'clock, although many of the larger stores in the city maintained the Western hours of opening and closing to accommodate the ever-increasing tourist market, for the Canaries were a duty-free zone, and thus attracted trade from many countries.

As far as shopping was concerned, the late afternoon opening of the stores meant a much later closing time, and this could have certain advantages for either the tourist or the working fraternity of the busy city.

Corinne and Joy sipped their coffee and gazed around them, fully savouring the cosmopolitan scene. A few tables away from them a pedlar was showing some tourists his wares which he extracted from an old battered suitcase for inspection, dangling what looked like gold bangles in front of the ladies. At another table a little way away from him, a small boy was trying to interest some more tourists into buying what looked like packets of bubble gum, and a small curly-haired girl beside him was offering packets of stamps.

The hopeful trading went on in a happy relaxed atmosphere and they moved on swiftly after receiving a dark glance from the table waiter as he circled the tables serving the customers.

When the waiter had gone back into the café to

collect the orders he had been given, the pedlars were back on their rounds, and from out of nowhere the man who had offered jewellery to the tourists a few tables away appeared at Corinne's table and proceeded to show them his wares. Bangles, brooches, and watches were held out for inspection, and Corinne and Joy politely shook their heads to show that they were not interested, but the man was looking at Juan, and to Corinne's embarrassment she found that Juan was looking at her as if seeking to ascertain if there was something that had caught her fancy. She then remembered the white carrier bag that now lay at Joy's feet and it occurred to her that perhaps Juan felt it necessary to buy something for her too.

Her abrupt shake of the head and firmed lips made it quite clear that she was not interested in any such gift, and even the hopeful pedlar got the message and moved on to ply his trade elsewhere.

Juan's mocking look at her told Corinne that he was well aware of her thoughts on the matter, and made her dislike him even more. The wretched man was altogether too knowing, she thought crossly, and centred her attention on a small knot of people that had gathered round a table at the back of the outdoor café's precincts. 'Dominoes,' Juan said dryly. 'It's a favourite occupation with the locals,' proving to Corinne that he was also aware of her wish to detach herself from his attention.

'Gambling?' asked a wide-eyed Joy.

Juan gave a light shrug. 'Sometimes,' he replied, still with his eyes on Corinne.

Corinne was pleased when he suggested that they resume their tour after they had finished their light lunch. She was beginning to feel the strain of Juan's constant observance, and wondered miserably if Joy had become aware of it, but when she called Corinne's attention to a clump of palms set in an oasis-like setting of the market area that they were just passing, Corinne doubted that she had; she was too enthralled by her surroundings.

The rest of that first day was spent in Las Palmas. Juan took them to the Plaza de Santa Ana, where the bronze statues of the heraldic dogs of Gran Canaria sat in dignified splendour flanking the front of St Anne's Cathedral. They did not visit the cathedral as Juan told them it would not be open until later that afternoon, but he promised them a visit at a later date.

It was in this section of the bustling city that the museums were to be found. There was the house-museum of Columbus, and, Juan recommended, well worth a visit for its historic contents. A short distance away was the Canary museum that specialised in anthropology and archaeology, also the island fauna. 'These are well worth seeing, and there are many interesting places to visit locally,' Juan remarked quietly, and Corinne felt rather than saw his swift glance towards her as he said this. He was no doubt fixing an itinerary for her, she thought sourly, on recalling their conversation the previous evening.

This section of the city was called Vegueta, and was the oldest part of Las Palmas. Juan called Corinne and Joy's attention to the narrowness of the streets —so narrow in fact that the cars that had parked there had had to take up part of the pavement to allow a passage through for other traffic.

The old houses with their small balconies told of the past, and it was easy to imagine *señoritas* peeping

over them with the proverbial rose in their carmined lips
that they would throw to the singing troubadour who
caught their fancy.

As they passed down the narrow streets, they
would suddenly get a glimpse of a hidden patio
behind gates of ornamental splendour, with bright
green ferns in raised urns, and various other exotic
flora. This reminded Corinne of Gabriel Mowbray's
house, and the intriguing glimpse she had had of
just such a garden, set as it were in the middle of the
house.

The gates through which these tantalising glimpses
could be seen were notable in themselves. Of fine
wrought iron, some were in gold and black, with
intricate designs of leaves and flowers of high work-
manship, probably as old as the houses themselves, and
proudly preserved.

So the day passed, and they finished the tour at the
Doramas Park, named, Juan told them, after one of the
Guanche kings.

This area of Las Palmas was the Ciudad Jardín or
Garden City, and was where the better endowed
Canarians lived in palatial splendour surrounded
by landscaped gardens. Through the foliage that
nestled against elaborately carved balconies could be
seen bright flashes of colour, mainly reds and pinks, but
as Juan explained, as warm as it was, it was still the
winter season, but within a few weeks these gardens
would be ablaze with colour, as would the gardens of
the hotel.

The Doramas Park, though small, contained some
fine examples of Canarian plant life. There were
many species of cacti, giant specimens of the small
potted variety to be bought in England, that soared

up towards the sky to tree-sized proportions.

There were tall stately palms, and a rather vicious-looking spike plant satirically named 'Mother-in-law's tongue'. Begonias were well to the fore, and lined the pathways in bright clusters of colour. Geraniums also, with their bright red and pink flowers, considerably enlivened what otherwise might have been a landscape of variegated greenery.

The park also contained a swimming pool, and a zoo, but these were not visited at that time. A little further on, Juan told them, was the Pueblo Canario, or Canarian village, built specifically to preserve local art and folklore, and where displays of folk dancing were held on certain days for the entertainment of the visitors, and Juan promised to take them to see the dancing that weekend.

By the time it was five o'clock, Corinne and Joy were ready to return to the hotel. They had seen a good part of the city, but this was mostly the tourist's tour, and there was much more to be seen, such as the shopping areas where the cosmopolitan trading of European and Asian products were sold side by side, and which promised a fascinating tour of discovery.

It was not until they were back at the hotel that Corinne realised just how tired they were. Joy fell on her bed as soon as she had entered her room and tossed the carrier bag towards Corinne. 'I hope you like the colour,' she said, stifling a yawn. 'I rather liked the darker blue, but Juan preferred the peacock blue.'

Corinne, about to go and collapse on her bed, gave an annoyed frown. 'That's just like him, isn't it?' she said crossly. 'You should have insisted on having the colour you liked—what is it, anyway?' she asked, hoping that it was not one of the caftans, but an embroidered blouse, perhaps, that she had seen Joy inspecting earlier.

'Oh, I had the colour I wanted,' Joy casually told her. 'It was yours he insisted on choosing the colour for.'

Corinne stared at her in consternation. 'Mine!' she exclaimed. 'For goodness' sake, Joy, you didn't let him buy me anything, did you?'

Joy gave a comical grimace. 'Can you see me stopping him?' she demanded. 'I had enough trouble trying to persuade him not to get me anything, but he went all haughty on me and made me feel awful.' She gave a wide grin. 'I've read about these masterful types, but I honestly didn't think they existed,' she added. 'You've got your work cut out there if you intend to throw that back at him,' she commented with a mischievous look in her eyes as she looked towards the carrier bag now at Corinne's feet.

Corinne's lips folded grimly as she picked the carrier up and removed its contents. They were caftans, of course, she might have known it, she thought furiously, and the more expensive ones, naturally, with gold braiding round the high collars and beautifully worked designs on the wide sleeves and around the hems.

One, as Joy had said, was of a heavenly peacock blue, and the other was an olive green. Made of a heavy silk material, they shimmered in the late afternoon light. 'Gorgeous, aren't they?' Joy said enthusiastically. 'It's probably Arabian silk. I must ask Carmen when we see her.' She lay back on her bed and put her arms behind her head. 'To think that the Sahara is just across the sea from here,' she breathed ecstatically. 'Did you hear what Juan said about the trading that goes on here between the East and the West? He said the port area is like the League of Nations. He said he's going to take us down there——'

She stopped when she saw that Corinne was not listening to her but staring dully at the caftans.

Corinne's thoughts were on her previous evening's confrontation with Juan and his answer to her query on his right to make her decisions for her. 'A husband's rights,' he had said in that soft silky way that she hated. Yet he had insisted that the marriage was a business deal only. You didn't buy clothes for your business partner, did you? she told herself bitterly. But then it was all a game to him, wasn't it? For all he knew she might have hated the colour he had chosen for her. She sighed deeply. If only he had chosen a deep red or some other colour that she heartily disliked, she could then have thrown it back at him in all honesty, but the peacock blue was a lovely colour and would certainly suit her.

Joy, who had been watching Corinne's changing expressions, suddenly asked, 'Will you wear it to that party the man we met was talking about?'

'Certainly not!' Corinne declared vehemently, with wide eyes. 'Just because he bought me a dress, it doesn't mean that I have to wear it, does it? I didn't ask him to buy me a dress, and as you so rightly commented, I can't very well give it back to him. No, I shall put it away in the wardrobe and forget it!'

'Coward!' Joy taunted at her. 'You'll look wonderful in it. It will suit you far better than the dark blue one I thought you'd like. I always said you ought to wear brighter colours, didn't I?'

Corinne did not reply, but gathered the dress up and went to her room, where she did exactly what she said that she would do and hung it at the back of the large roomy wardrobe, then shut the wardrobe doors firmly in an action that proclaimed finality on her part over the whole episode.

During tea, however, it was not so easy to dismiss the gift of the dress and, fuming, Corinne knew she would have to say something about it. Joy had no doubt given her thanks at the time the gift had been made, and that left her in the obnoxious position of having to say thank you for a gift she had neither sought nor wanted. To say 'Thank you, but you shouldn't have bothered,' would sound trite and ungracious, and as annoyed as she was, she could not say that. In the end she settled for a stiff-sounding, 'Thank you for the gift,' and left it at that, aware the whole time of Joy's amused eyes and equally amused thoughts.

Juan's autocratic eyebrows raised as he accepted the tea she had just poured out for him. 'Wear it tomorrow evening,' he commented casually, but Corinne knew that he was giving her an order, an order that she was to obey without argument.

Her fuming eyes met his cold grey ones as she handed him a plate of finely cut sandwiches, and the hand holding the plate shook slightly as she tried to control her temper, and it was all she could do not to throw the plate at him.

'It will suit you,' he went on calmly, and before Corinne could reply he turned his attention to Joy who was trying to look as if food was the only thing on her mind and was helping herself to another sandwich. 'I'm afraid the hours will be too late for you,

Joy, but no doubt there will be a few barbecues in the near future.'

Joy gave him a smile that made Corinne wonder once again whose side she was on. 'Oh, don't worry about me,' she replied happily. 'I hate parties, and I want to do some sketches for Carmen to look at when she visits again,' she declared with a note of contentment in her voice.

Juan excused himself after tea, leaving a still fuming Corinne and a thoroughly absorbed Joy working out a few designs in her mind ready to commit to paper. 'I wonder if there's anything around that I could use for sketching,' she said dreamily, not realising that her loving sister was harbouring unloving thoughts towards her traitorous acceptance of the way her new brother-in-law was stamping his authority on her sister, regardless of her feelings in the matter.

'No doubt you've only to ask, and it will be provided,' Corinne replied bitterly, knowing it was no use slating Joy for Juan's behaviour; she had no one but herself to blame for the mess she was in, and could only hope that in time she would be able to accept Juan's dictatorial attitude towards her with as much placidity as Joy did, unquestioningly accepting him as master of this new domain. Her soft lips firmed on this thought, for she could not envisage herself ever accepting such a role. She had had to fend for Joy and herself for too long to just hand over the reins and sit back and enjoy the ride—a ride that was inevitably to take her over very bumpy ground, and she didn't even know where she was heading, or what lay at the end of the journey. She glanced back at Joy, now idly folding her serviette into pleats but with her mind far away. At least she was happy, Corinne thought, and surely that was enough to be going on with. Her frown deepened. Juan Martel held the whip-hand now, but should he make Joy un-happy—Corinne's small chin lifted and her dark blue eyes blazed—she would make him rue the day he ever set eyes on her, let alone forced her to marry him!

CHAPTER EIGHT

AFTER dinner that evening, Carmen made a welcome visit. Welcome, because an oppressive atmosphere had prevailed throughout the meal. Joy for once was quiet, wrapped up in her own world of designs, for Juan had promised to supply her with the drawing paper she required, and which had been delivered shortly before dinner and she was longing to get down to work.

It was up to Corinne to keep the conversation go-ing, but although she tried hard to forget her latest grievance over the way she had been ordered to wear the dress Juan had bought for her, it still rankled, and all her replies to his questions were stiff-sounding and over-polite.

When he introduced her to the various dishes laid out for their consumption, explaining how fish made up a good proportion of the daily fare, for there was an abundance of seafood to be had on the island, Corinne hoped that her expression of polite interest successfully hid her innermost thoughts, for while she listened, her dark blue eyes scrutinised the hard features of the stranger she had married.

If he was aware of this scrutiny he gave no sign of it, but there was a certain look lurking at the back of his grey eyes that made Corinne concentrate a little harder on what he was telling her than she might otherwise have done.

Carmen's arrival was extremely well timed, as far as Corinne was concerned anyway, and Joy of course was just as pleased to see her, but for a different reason.

When the women settled down to chat, Juan left them to it with an amused, 'One, maybe two, I can take in my stride, but three's enough to call my urgent attention elsewhere!'

'Look who's always telling me I can't leave the business!' Carmen called towards his vanishing back, and then turned back to the sisters with a satisfied smile. 'He's right, of course, and he wouldn't be interested in our gossip. Now what have you seen today?' she asked.

'We went to that market you spoke about,' Joy answered swiftly, and got up. 'Juan bought us a caftan each. I'll show you mine,' and going to get it she cast a wicked look at Corinne as she left the room. 'Corinne's hidden hers, but if you speak to her nicely, I expect she'll show you it!' she said gaily.

Corinne frowned at the door Joy had just gone through, then turned to find Carmen's amused eyes on her. 'The gift annoyed you, then?' she asked with a certain amount of interest in her voice.

Corinne held her hands up in a gesture that said more than words. 'I didn't want him to buy me anything,' she said quietly, only realising how odd that must have sounded to Carmen, for Juan was her husband, but it was too late to retract her words now, and she was only thankful that Juan was not present to witness her confusion.

To her relief, Carmen did not comment on this, but gave Corinne a sympathetic smile and leant over towards her and patted her arm in a motherly way. 'Juan's a law unto himself,' she said softly. 'Accept him as he is, my dear. Don't fight him, you won't win. He's too used to getting his own way.'

Corinne's wondering eyes searched Carmen's earnest brown ones. If her statement had been slightly odd, then Carmen's had been even odder, and it occurred to Corinne that she had made her own deductions over the sudden marriage of her stepson, and for one awful second Corinne wondered if she knew the truth and looked away hastily and stared at her hands now clasped tightly together.

Had Juan told her? she wondered miserably, and if so, what must she think of her? Let alone the despicable part she had played in ascertaining Clair's inheritance.

By that time Joy had returned with the caftan, and she and Carmen went into a huddle over the material, leaving Corinne to her own musings, and it was only after she had recalled that Carmen had known nothing of the marriage at their first meeting that she was able to breathe a sigh of relief, for there had been no opportunity for Carmen to have a private word with Juan since then, and it was hardly a subject to be discussed over the telephone!

The evening sped by, and at ten-thirty Joy was finding it hard to keep awake, although she hated to admit it. Carmen, however, sent her off to bed with a promise that she would offer to take them on the tour of the shopping centre, an offer, she said with a smile, that would be gratefully accepted by Juan.

To Corinne's annoyance Joy, before she went to bed, again mentioned the caftan that Corinne had tucked away in her wardrobe, saying, 'Show it to Carmen, Corinne. I'm sure she'll agree that you ought to wear it to that party Juan's going to take you to,' then blew her a kiss and left.

At the mention of a party, Carmen looked interested. 'Whose party?' she queried, and Corinne told her of the meeting that morning with Miguel Blanco and the subsequent invitation.

'And Juan agreed?' asked Carmen with raised brows, adding half to herself, 'That's odd.'

Corinne gave a light shrug. 'He said something about someone called Dolores wanting to meet me,' she added, and was surprised at Carmen's reaction to this.

'Not very kind of him,' remarked Carmen, her brown eyes narrowed in speculation. 'But that's Juan. He doesn't believe in half measures.'

Corinne, who had no idea what Carmen was talking about, had to agree with this, and her eyes held a spark of amusement in them as they met Carmen's thoughtful ones.

'Don't get too chummy with Dolores, Corinne,' Carmen said suddenly, surprising Corinne with her earnestness. 'I like you, and I don't want you to get hurt. She considers Juan her personal property, and you'll be very lucky if she doesn't throw the wine decanter at you.' She paused in thought for a second before adding dryly, 'Although no doubt she will manage to contain herself in Juan's presence, but make no mistake, you have an enemy there.'

Corinne's frank blue eyes met Carmen's slightly worried ones. 'In that case I see what you mean by it not being very kind of Juan to take me to meet her,' she said quietly. 'I shall feel very sorry for her,' she added slowly.

'Good gracious, Corinne!' exclaimed Carmen, 'it's you I'm worried about, not Dolores. She and Juan are one of a kind, both are quite capable of looking after themselves.' She gave Corinne a quick assessing look. 'You're not in love with Juan, are you?' she stated flatly.

Corinne's eyes widened at this, and before she could stop herself she had exclaimed indignantly, 'Of course not!' Then as the implication of her words sank through to her she stared back at Carmen, who was not at all put out by this bald statement. 'You knew it was not a real marriage, didn't you?' she asked with a hint of curiosity in her voice.

Carmen shrugged expressively. 'Because I know Juan,' she replied slowly. 'And because he's in love with Dolores,' she added simply. 'I don't know how he got you to marry him,' she gave a slight grimace, 'and however he managed it, I don't think I want to know, but I do know why he married you. He was punishing Dolores for disobeying his orders and joining some friends of hers on a cruise.' She gave another expressive shrug. 'She must have just got back, hence the reason for the party, but she didn't bargain on such a shock as Juan's marriage on her arrival home,' she added significantly.

Corinne stared back at Carmen, then blinked in disbelief. 'Surely he wouldn't go that far—not as far as to ma——' she stopped here as the thought struck her that he would go that far, in fact had!

Carmen nodded slowly. 'Oh, yes, he would, and he did, didn't he?' she replied. 'Dolores ought to have known better than to flaunt his wishes, but I think she was tired of waiting for him to marry her. She's a widow, you see. She married a man much older than herself. It was an arranged marriage, of course, with a well-endowed family. I don't like her,' she declared abruptly, 'but it couldn't have been easy for her, tied to an older man. It's hardly a year since her husband died, and Juan's a stickler for protocol, that's why he was against her going on that cruise, knowing the people she was going with, a set of pleasure-loving wealthy drifters. He was furious when she defied him.'

Carmen's gaze left Corinne and she stared at the richly carpeted floor at her feet. 'As I said, I heartily dislike Dolores, but I can understand her wanting a little freedom, especially after a marriage like that.'

Corinne gave a little shudder of sympathy for the woman who had married a man she did not love, and although she was in the same position, at least it was not a true marriage, and there was no fear of any other implication on the part of either of them to alter this status quo. 'Surely if Juan loves her, he would understand her feelings,' Corinne answered indignantly. 'Why couldn't he have joined her on that cruise?' Her soft mouth twisted ironically as she added, 'Too caught up with business affairs, I suppose.'

Carmen shot her a swift look. 'Can you see him accepting someone else's arrangements?' She gave a slow shake of the head. 'Not Juan!' she stated emphatically. 'Dolores' small taste of freedom must have gone to her head, or she would never have defied him like that.' She put her head on one side and stared at Corinne assessingly. 'Don't fall in love with Juan, Corinne,' she said quietly, 'you'll only get badly hurt. As I said earlier, I do not think it was very kind of him to throw you into the fray so quickly.' She frowned. 'I wish——' then she stopped abruptly, and gave a small grimace. 'I wish I could offer you a job, Corinne, that way I could keep an eye on you, but at least I have Joy, and a perfect excuse for keeping in close touch with the pair of you. Just remember what I said about not getting involved heartwise with Juan, and try to give Dolores a wide berth whenever possible. It's their private fight, and I see no reason why you should get mauled in the skirmish.'

Corinne gave Carmen a smile that lit up her lovely eyes and made Carmen begin to feel a little sorry for Dolores, and extremely angry with Juan for bringing this lovely, unsophisticated creature into his harsh reckonings with Dolores. 'I have no intention of getting involved with either of them,' Corinne replied steadily, 'at least,' she amended slowly, 'not in the way that you're worried about.' Her eyes narrowed in thought. 'I can see, though, that I'm in for a stormy passage, but thanks to you, I shall be able to sidestep most of it now that I understand the plot.' She gave Carmen a grateful look. 'I won't have to worry over Joy, either, thanks to you,' she added sincerely.

Carmen gave an abrupt nod and stood up. 'Well, I had better be on my way,' she said, smothering a sudden yawn of tiredness. 'Juan will be back shortly and will be offering me a bed,' she gave a smile at the thought, then as she walked to the door she turned back towards Corinne again. 'One other thing, Corinne,' she said softly. 'Don't try to cross Juan, no matter how infuriating he can be, even though there'll be times when you'll want to throw the furniture at him. He's very like his father,' she gave a soft sigh. 'I adored him, but there were times—' she smiled, 'well, anyway, just agree with him and play it his way. A soothing "yes" will work wonders in your relationship.'

Corinne's sceptical eyes met Carmen's as she replied ironically. 'You mean, "Yes, master", don't you?'

Carmen's answering chuckle echoed around the lounge long after she had gone, and Corinne sighed deeply. It wasn't funny at all, she thought, and although she felt grateful to Carmen for putting her in the picture, she now wished that she had been left in ignorance.

In time, of course, she would have found out the truth behind Juan's sudden decision to marry her. If Clair had come to Gran Canaria as she should have done, no doubt she would now be in the same position as Corinne was. Her soft lips twisted, in spite of what he had said about preferring Corinne's simplicity to Clair's sophistication. It was a case of a bird in the hand was worth two in the bush, she thought bitterly. He would have realised that Clair could have become a millstone around his neck. No, he had left nothing to chance, and with Joy's future at stake, he held all the trumps.

Corinne went to her room when she thought she heard Juan returning. She could not bear to face him at that moment in time. What he had done to her was bad enough, but what he was doing to the woman he apparently loved was even worse, because she would not know that the marriage was in name only, and would go through an agony of emotions.

If that was love, then she wanted no part of it, Corinne told herself firmly as she prepared herself for bed. On recalling Carmen's advice on not falling for Juan, she gave a small snort of indignation. How could anyone fall in love with a man like that? A man who would not only rule your life but intrude upon your thoughts as well, like some sort of mind-reader. An altogether too knowing character for Corinne's liking. Oh, no, there was absolutely no danger of her succumbing to his charms—if he possessed any, and she was extremely doubtful that he did!

Good looks and suave manner did not amount to charm in her reckoning, and Corinne thanked her lucky stars that she was able to see this where others might have been blinded by the sheer forceful personality of the man.

Just before she fell asleep Corinne told herself drowsily that she ought to be grateful for the fact that Juan Martel's hard heart had been firmly captured by another woman, and in time he would surely seek the annulment he had said he would be applying for. She fell asleep on the thought that it would all work out for him. He would make certain of that, and with a little luck things would work out for her too. She might even yet find herself joining Joy in Carmen's business.

CHAPTER NINE

THE following day Carmen took Corinne and Joy on a tour of the shopping areas of the city. As Carmen had intimated, Juan was only too happy to let her take over this chore, and to Corinne's relief did not offer to accompany them, removing any fears that she might have had of him buying any other unwanted gifts, where she was concerned, anyway, for Joy had been pleased enough with the gift of the caftan.

The first area visited was the Triana high street, which was the commercial centre of the city, and here, as Corinne gazed down the length of the long street, she was struck by the European influence of neon-lighted signs above the trading premises. These were numerous and of varying sizes, all proclaiming a commercial interest in whatever one was tempted to buy.

In spite of the blatancy of these signs, there was a general air of bustling prosperity that both Corinne and Joy found invigorating, and added to this was the constant expectancy of coming across some exotic wares only to be found in that part of the world.

There were, of course, many products from Europe, but it was in the shops that catered mainly for the tourist trade that one found such unusual items as baby sharks bottled in a greyish fluid and suspended in time—perfect replicas of their kind, and although Corinne knew that sharks could be dangerous, she felt a tinge of sadness at the sight.

They wandered from window to window, gazing with delight at the jewellers shops displaying bowls of uncut stones that glimmered softly in the light, and Carmen told them that there were bargains to be had in uncut stones.

The fur shops also produced a few surprises price-wise, and Corinne thought of Clair as she gazed at a gorgeous red fox fur, only half the price that one would have paid in England.

When Carmen said that they would call in at her place for coffee, Joy's day was complete, for Corinne knew she had been hoping for just such a chance to see the premises where she would shortly be employed.

To Corinne and Joy's surprise, Carmen led them to a heavily studded door that was another reminder of the past glories of Spanish occupation, set in between a jewellers and a bookstore, and once inside, led them up a wide staircase discreetly carpeted in maroon.

The walls were white and completely unadorned, and all the more striking because of this, for the banisters were elegantly engraved in gold filigree tracings of leaves and no additional trappings were required.

Corinne felt Joy glance at her as they mounted the staircase, and she could guess her thoughts. Hardly the entrance to a boutique—at least not the kind of boutique they had been accustomed to! After what Juan had told her, Corinne was not so astounded as Joy was, and she had purposely not forewarned Joy, thinking of the delightful surprise she would receive when she took up her new position.

At the end of a long corridor they came to double glass doors on which was inscribed in gold lettering, 'Estillo', and as Carmen pushed them open and smiled a welcoming admittance to the girls, Joy's nervousness was very apparent and Corinne had to push her forward.

If anything, Joy's nervousness increased as they moved forward into what seemed another world— a world of fashion, luxurious and utterly dedicated.

In one corner of the large room was a desk, at that moment unoccupied, but as they walked towards it a woman materialised from behind a velvet curtained-off section and glided rather than walked towards them, favouring Carmen with a ready smile.

'Ah, Marcia, could you arrange for us to have some coffee, please,' Carmen requested. 'We've been window-shopping, and I for one am exhausted!' She gave a contented sigh as she moved towards a door on her right. 'Come into my domain,' she said, 'we shall be undisturbed there.'

Carmen's 'domain' turned out to be her office, a large and very cluttered room with rolls of expensive-looking material lying half spread out on a bench against a window, as if waiting for some use to be found for them. Sheets of foolscap with designs doodled on them lay in glorious disorder on the heavy desk at which Carmen seated herself with an airy wave towards a group of elegant-looking chairs opposite the desk, indicating that they should make themselves comfortable. 'This is where we go into our huddles,' she commented with a wide smile, and looked at Joy, who had still not quite recovered at finding herself in such impressive premises. 'Well, how do you think you will like working here?' she asked her with a trace of anxiousness in her voice, for Joy had been remarkably silent since they had entered the salon.

Joy swallowed and uttered a dry-sounding, 'Fine,' but seemed incapable of enlarging on this.

Corinne came to her rescue with an amused, 'You did say it was a boutique, you know, and so we——' she gave a half-shrug and left the rest unsaid.

Carmen's eyebrows lifted and then she caught the drift of Corinne's message. 'Oh, dear!' she said, and gave a comical moue. 'We have a boutique, of course, but it's only in its infancy. This is where the real work is done.' She gave Joy an apologetic look. 'And now you're worried, aren't you? You've no cause to worry, you know. You will not be thrown into the work until you're ready,' she waved an airy hand towards the material on the bench. 'This is where we play around with ideas, and we could do with some bright new brains. You'll be able to create to your heart's content, but first I want you to get the feel of the business. I shall want you to assist Marcia in the fitting rooms for a start—now you won't mind that, will you?' she queried gently. 'It will not take you long to learn the rules of the house. For instance, from time to time we get new patronage from someone who happened to admire one of our dresses, and wants exactly the same style for herself, but this we do not allow, we would not be in business very long if we did. No, we offer to dress Madame in suitable but individual clothes.'

She stopped here as the office door opened. 'Ah, here's our coffee—Juan! For goodness' sake! What are you doing here?' she exclaimed, as the tall form of Corinne's husband entered the room.

'You've no objection, I trust, to my taking my wife
to lunch?' he asked dryly. 'I had an idea you might
end up here.' He gave Corinne a disturbingly possessive look. 'I suggest we leave these two to their business affairs. Are you ready?' he requested in a tone
that said that she had better be.

Corinne could only give a silent nod and gather her
handbag off the floor where she had laid it beside her
chair, and stand up.

'Really, Juan!' began Carmen in a highly indignant
voice, but on meeting Juan's eyes she gave a light
shrug and said, 'Well, enjoy your lunch, Corinne.
I'll see Joy gets back to the hotel,' and left it at that.

As Juan escorted her through the salon, and down
the staircase towards the main street, Corinne felt
like a bought slave, she could even feel the shackles
around her wrists! She knew very well why Juan
had decided to take her to lunch, indeed take her
anywhere, out of Carmen's business interests. Telling her, and Carmen, come to that, that he had no intention of letting her get personally involved in that
or any other business.

Carmen was right, she thought bitterly, you could
not fight a man like that, not if you wanted a peaceful existence, and Corinne did want a peaceful life;
the alternative was too miserable to contemplate.

The restaurant that Juan had chosen to take her to
for lunch was within walking distance of the salon,
and as they entered the slightly darkened entrance
of the restaurant, the rich velvet curtaining cutting
off the bright sunlight, Corinne decided to follow
Carmen's advice. It was not going to be easy for her,
she knew, but somehow she must adopt a more con-

ciliatory attitude towards this dominant man. Joy was happy, and it was Joy who really mattered, and she had no doubt now whatsoever that he would do exactly what he had threatened to do if she continued to annoy him. If he could treat the woman he loved to such harsh treatment, then he would not hesitate to exact an equally hard judgment on two comparative strangers, even though they were his wife and sister-in-law!

Corinne gave a slight shudder at this thought and Juan, closely watching her as the waiter seated her at the table he had led them to, remarked, 'You are not in a draught, are you?'

This produced a look of consternation on the waiter's face as he looked at Corinne, and she hastened to reassure both of them that no, she was not in a draught, it was probably the fact that they had come in from brilliant sunshine, and really, the coolness of the restaurant was refreshing.

Satisfied with this, the waiter then took their order which Juan gave in Spanish, and to which the waiter listened to with what appeared to be almost reverent attention, and his, '*Si*, Señor Martel,' proved that Juan was known to him.

While they waited for the lunch to be served, Juan poured Corinne a glass of the light wine that he had chosen as an aperitif, and while she sipped it she gazed around at the restaurant, in fact anywhere but directly at the man seated opposite her.

'Joy will be happy with Carmen, don't you think?' he said musingly, not allowing Corinne's interest to stray away from him.

Corinne, who had been looking at a huge picture on the wall at the end of the restaurant, gave a start and reluctantly tore her gaze away from a pair of Spanish dancers depicted in the picture, and looked at Juan. 'Oh, I'm sure she will be,' she replied quietly. 'She wasn't expecting quite such a grand set-up, though,' she added, with a touch of amusement in her voice as she recalled Joy's nervous reaction at her first glimpse of the salon.

Juan's grey eyes searched Corinne's as she made this reply. It was the first time that they had had what might be called a normal conversation since they had met each other—normal, that was, in the sense that there was no resentment on either side.

It would have been better if it had been left at that, but Juan's next question threw the almost calm Corinne back into a state of flux, and she was instantly on her guard willing herself not to lose her temper. 'And you,' he had asked softly, 'with me?'

Her flushed cheeks and the blue sparks that flew out of her eyes gave their own answer, but she managed to reply calmly enough. 'That depends,' she said slowly.

'On what?' he demanded challengingly, and his eyes narrowed as his glance flicked casually over her. 'I shall not change my mind and allow you to take up an occupation, at least not a business one. Apart from that, I see no reason why you should not be perfectly happy with your situation,' he stated haughtily, then stared down at the table. 'In time,' he added significantly, 'changes will be made that will be more to your liking. It will be a question of patience on both sides, but mainly yours,' he said meaningly.

Corinne's thoughts were on the annulment when he said this, and she felt an instant surge of relief.

'In that case I will be patient,' she replied lightly, and somewhat thankfully.

She did not quite understand Juan's silent amusement at this, for he made no comment, but his eyes laughed at her and she wondered why.

Lunch was then served, and it was not until they had reached the coffee stage that Juan mentioned the party that they would be attending that evening. 'You will be meeting several friends of mine,' he began as he handed Corinne the cream jug, 'people I have known for many years, and I shall want you to be especially vigilant. It will be necessary to give the impression that the marriage is a real one, you understand?' And at Corinne's quick nod of comprehension, he went on, 'As I said before, no outward demonstration of affection will be required, apart from my casually placing my arm around your waist while we talk to people. That of course will be expected—we are to all intents and purposes still on honeymoon, remember.'

He gave Corinne a hard look. 'I shall not expect you to push my arm away, or jump out of reaching distance, or give me one of those extremely provocative looks of yours, that declare your abhorrence of the situation, either,' he added meaningly. His firm lips twisted. 'They are provocative, you know, and have quite the opposite effect on me. Perhaps one day I will answer the challenge that you issue out of those lovely eyes of yours, and you will learn to mask your thoughts.'

Corinne's eyes opened wide as she stared back at him wondering how on earth the conversation had reached this embarrassing stage. She understood perfectly what was required of her, and although she did not see herself as a good actress she had been willing to try. 'Thank you for the compliment,' she replied stiffly, in a manner that said she did not consider it a compliment at all. 'I can only promise to do my best, but I'm not very good at duplicity, and I'm certainly not issuing a challenge when I'm outraged,' she added furiously, tacking on for good measure, 'but I do see the wisdom of keeping my thoughts to myself!'

Juan's grim expression changed to an amused one, and his white teeth gleamed as he gave Corinne a wicked smile. 'You'll try, of course, but I doubt that you'll succeed, not with me.'

Corinne took a deep breath and was about to give a very decisive answer to this taunting remark when she realised that Juan was enjoying himself at her expense. 'I'm glad you're amused,' she said bitterly. 'It's all a game to you, isn't it?' she demanded. 'You really should have chosen Clair, you know, she wouldn't have needed any prompting.'

'She wouldn't, would she,' Juan agreed maddeningly, 'but I chose you—for beter, for worse, remember?' he quoted softly, making Corinne look hastily away from the mocking light in his eyes, as she felt her cheeks grow warm.

Later that evening as she dressed for the party, Corinne listened abstractedly to Joy's pleased comments on how she knew the caftan would suit her and how right Juan had been in insisting on that certain colour, as it brought out the golden lights in her hair and emphasised the dark blue of her eyes.

Corinne had just nodded and continued to brush her hair. Her thoughts were on her last encounter with Juan and his remarks in regard to their marriage, particularly the 'for better or for worse' comment, as if the marriage had been a real one and he had no thought of an annulment.

She thought of the evening ahead of her, and her soft lips firmed. It had been his way of assuring her full co-operation, of this she was certain, but what manner of man was he to exact such punishment for what was only a natural act of defiance on the part of a woman who sought a little freedom from the confines of a loveless marriage?

Corinne shook her head slowly. And he had criticised her for her part in what he had looked on as a plot to ensure Clair's inheritance. What he was asking her to do now was even more despicable. Gabriel Mowbray had died happy, content that his will would be carried out, and it had been, although not quite according to the rule book. But what about Dolores? How many months of torture was Juan going to inflict upon her?

'Your hair's fine,' exclaimed Joy impatiently, noting the way Corinne was fairly vigorously punishing it with the hairbrush. 'Come and see what Carmen sent over for you to wear with the dress,' and she pulled Corinne off the dressing table chair and into her room where on the bed lay a white fur coat. 'You shall go to the ball, Cinderella,' she said gaily, as she picked it up off the bed and gave it to Corinne, sweeping the soft luxurious fur around her shoulders in a triumphant gesture.

Corinne had meant to wear a white fluffy cardigan over the dress, for although the days were warm, the evenings could be chilly. 'We'll get above ourselves at this rate,' commented Corinne, trying to make the remark lighthearted; but she felt embarrassed by the gift and had it been given by anyone else but Carmen she would have refused it.

'Carmen said it's a late wedding present,' Joy went on with shining eyes. 'I say, Corinne, I do like her, and she's frightfully successful, you know, but not a bit proud. I know I'm going to love the job,' she added with a misty note in her voice.

That was all Corinne needed to ensure that she did not fail in her task that evening. So let Juan put his arm around her waist, he could even kiss her—she baulked a little at this thought, and her knees were not quite as steady as they had been before as she walked towards the lounge to join him ready for their departure. As she settled herself in his car, and noted the grim expression on his hard face, she was comforted by the fact that he had said that there would be no exhibition of outward affection between them, apart from his placing a casual arm around her waist, so there was really nothing for her to worry about.

The car purred along the busy streets and Corinne noticed that they were going towards the Ciudad Jardín area, where the wealthier citizens of Las Palmas lived in large palatial residences surrounded by landscaped gardens.

Her nervousness increased as the car eventually swept up a long curving drive bordered by thick shrubbery and soon they were in sight of a well-lighted patio in front of an imposing-looking house, and Juan brought the car to a swishing stop next to several others that were parked along the front of the house.

When she entered the house with Juan's strong hand on her arm, Corinne wished with all her heart

that Joy or Carmen were with her. She had never
felt so entirely alone in all her life, and desperately
wished that Juan would say something, anything, but
he remained silent the whole time, thinking, Corinne
surmised miserably, of Dolores.

If he was miserable, then it served him right,
Corinne thought bitterly. That was the strange thing
about hurting someone you loved; you hurt yourself too, even more than the other person.

The room they entered appeared to be full of
people, and Corinne gave a quick nervous glance towards Juan as they walked to join the assembly, and
his answer was a swift hardening grip on her arm,
as if warning her not to give way to nerves.

Corinne did not know whether it was her imagination or not, but she sensed a slight hush upon their
entry, but the next moment everybody started talking again and the gay, frivolous chatter that marks
such occasions filled the room.

It was not long before they were in the middle of
a huddle of guests, all anxious to be introduced to
Juan's English wife, and as the names were reeled
out, Corinne was amazed to hear Juan call her
Corinne and not Clair, and although she was pleas-
antly surprised by this condescension on his part, she
was also aware of his determination to see the whole
wretched thing through.

During all these introductions and the polite yet
obviously curious looks she was receiving, Corinne
steeled herself to meet Dolores, who must be somewhere in the room, but as the room, as large as it was,
was so crowded, it was just possible that she had not
seen their entry.

Corinne darted a quick look at Juan, and while

absently noting how handsome he looked, even more devastating in evening wear, she thought, she saw that he was smiling at something that someone had said, his strong white teeth gleaming against his dark features, and again she was reminded of his strength, and his cruelty. She felt bewildered too, for she could not believe that he was suffering in any way, and surely he should have been suffering, not looking as if he was thoroughly enjoying himself.

She was warned of Dolores' presence by Juan's arm that was placed possessively around her waist as a dark-haired beauty approached them with a husky, 'Juan! How long have you been here? You're usually the last to arrive!'

The words were said in an amused-sounding way, yet Corinne took particular notice that the woman's dark eyes did not echo the lightness of her tone, and while she spoke to Juan they remained fixed on Corinne. 'So you took the plunge at last,' she went on, now transferring her gaze back to Juan. 'While my back was turned too, how very unkind of you,' she added, pouting her full red lips at him. 'You must tell me all about it. Come, we shall catch up on our news in solitude.' She held out an elegant lace-sleeved arm for Juan to take.

'I think not,' Juan answered quietly, declining the very obvious invitation for a private tête-à-tête with her, and drawing Corinne even closer to his side. 'Corinne, this is Señora Dolores Galdós, and our hostess this evening. Dolores, this is Corinne, my wife. I took the plunge readily enough,' he commented dryly, and lifted one of Corinne's small hands to his firm lips. 'And who could blame me?' he added, as his lips caressed the palm of Corinne's hand, making her want to snatch her hand away, but Juan's grip was very firm, and so was the look in his eyes as they met Corinne's.

'How very quaint,' Dolores commented, as her watchful eyes took in the delicate flush on Corinne's cheeks at Juan's action. 'I think I can see the attraction,' she said lightly, making Corinne's flush deepen as she caught the implication behind her words, reminding Corinne of a certain remark of Juan's shortly after their marriage, that he was tired of sophisticated women. Her knowing glance and her instant dismissal of Corinne as a rival made Corinne dislike her intensely, and she could understand Carmen's feelings on the matter.

The hand that Juan still held disguisedly lightly against his lips trembled slightly, and Corinne prayed that he would put her agitation down to temper, and not to fear, for those firm lips of his were awakening a response from her heart, a heart as yet unscathed by the traumas of love. Not that Corinne realised this, she only knew that her bones seemed to be turning to jelly and that she felt most peculiar.

Having dismissed Corinne, Dolores fixed her dark eyes on Juan, clearly issuing a challenge as she remarked casually, 'Do circulate, we can't have you hogging each other's company all evening, can we?' and moved gracefully away to join another group of guests.

Corinne's eyes followed Dolores' slim back as she walked away, and she was disturbed to find that her hand was still held by Juan when she looked back at him, and he was looking at her and not in Dolores' direction. For a ghastly moment Corinne wondered if he had mistaken the cause of her agitation, but when he smiled at her and murmured, 'Well done!' her heartbeats slowed down, not quite back to normal, but at least to a manageable tattoo.

When he lowered her hand, Corinne's relief was shortlived, because he did not release it but held it firmly in his as he commented dryly, 'So, we circulate,' and led her to a small knot of people grouped in the opposite direction to where Dolores was standing. 'We shall not be expected to stay long,' Juan said dryly, as they neared the group, 'not on our honeymoon, as it were,' he added.

Corinne's heartbeats went back to the rhythm of the posthorn gallop, and she wondered furiously if he was doing it on purpose; it was his beloved he was supposed to be plaguing, not her! If he was doing it on purpose, then she doubted her ability to stay the course!

In the meantime she did her best to enter into the spirit of the party, but it was not easy, for Juan seemed to find plenty of occasions in which to slip his arm around her slim waist, and Corinne was not at all sure that so many demonstrations of outward affection were entirely necessary, but she was grateful for the fact that he did not kiss her hand again.

By the time it was eleven o'clock, her head was aching with the unaccustomed noise of laughter and loud conversation, and she vaguely wondered why people always seemed to talk that much louder at such parties, and she suspected that it was the liberal doses of alcohol consumed that produced this effect.

To Juan's annoyance Miguel Blanco—who it appeared was Dolores' brother—had attached himself to their party, and constantly hovered around Corinne. Corinne suspected that it was his intention to wrench her from Juan's side whenever the opportunity presented itself. The reason for such a move was not so hard to guess at, she reasoned silently, sure that he was under orders from his sister, who must by now be grinding her teeth in frustration at her inability to manoeuvre a private word with Juan.

It was then that fate lent Dolores a helping hand, as Juan was asked to take a telephone call, which he took in the adjoining room, and by closing the door he could hear what was said on the other end of the line without having to ask for silence from the more rowdy section of the company.

Having received a distinct order from Juan to stay where she was before he went to take the call, Corinne was not surprised to find Miguel beside her within seconds of the door closing behind Juan.

'Let me get you some more sherry,' he said, attempting to take the half-empty glass Corinne was holding, and had been nursing for most of the evening, successfully dodging the attendant waiter's efforts to keep all the glasses filled.

Corinne smiled as she declined the offer. 'No, thank you,' she said, 'I've reached my limit.'

It was just at that moment that she caught sight of Dolores entering the room that Juan had gone into to take the call, and her eyes remained fixed on the door as it closed silently behind her.

Her first thought was that Juan would be furious at her intrusion, but then it occurred to her that perhaps he had arranged the whole set-up. He was not likely to miss the chance of observing Dolores' true reaction to his marriage.

Miguel had followed Corinne's gaze and gave a

deep sigh. 'I'm afraid your marriage was a great shock for Dolores,' he said in a funereal voice, that was not echoed in his light brown eyes as they met Corinne's frank gaze, and she had the impression that he was secretly enjoyng himself. She also knew with certainty that he did not care for his sister, and this was perhaps the reason for his rather puckish attitude.

'I hope I'm not speaking out of turn,' he went on, still in that doleful voice, 'but you're sure to hear rumours about them.' He gave another exaggerated sigh, 'I'm sure you won't begrudge her a few minutes alone with your husband, will you?'

Corinne's eyebrows rose at this, and she wondered what her answer would have been if she had been madly in love with Juan. As it was, she simply said, 'Of course not,' and left it at that.

Their attention was then directed to a pair of heavily built men who were having an altercation that looked like turning into a serious fight at any moment.

'Diego and Salvador,' commented Miguel, with an odd twisted smile. 'Don't worry, it's not as bad as it looks. They're brothers and business partners, and really enjoy a disagreement.'

As he said this, the first blow was struck and the recipient staggered back against an occasional table that went crashing to the floor.

'Well, it doesn't usually get this far,' Miguel said with a frown, and caught Corinne's arm, 'I think perhaps it might be better if I escort you into the garden until things are brought to order. Juan would never forgive me if you became embroiled in a brawl,' and he led Corinne to the French windows and out into the cool fresh evening air.

Corinne's thoughts on this protective action of
Miguel's in regard to Juan's feelings would have surprised Miguel had he been privileged to hear them, for
she was certain that nothing short of the house falling
down would have disturbed either Juan or the woman
he loved, as she envisaged them wrapped in each other's
arms.

If all went well, she told herself, Juan would be
pressing for that annulment within a matter of
weeks, and surely he would be so happy that he
would not mind if Corinne elected to stay in the
Canaries. It was not as if she would cause him any
embarrassment, for their paths need never cross
again.

These thoughts should have lifted Corinne up to
the skies, but she felt only a deep sadness, and she
was shocked and surprised at her feelings. What was
the matter with her? Had that wretched man so
bullied her that she was now incapable of fending
for herself again? She gave a swift nod at this explanation. It had to be that; she simply refused to
believe that she had fallen in love with a man who had
used her in such a despicable way only to hurt the
woman he really loved.

Miguel led her to a stone bench in an alcove at
the side of the house, and considerately brushed away
any dust or debris that might have been on the seat
with his silk handkerchief, before allowing her to be
seated.

If only to stop the trend of such thoughts that
threatened to envelop her very existence, Corinne
asked Miguel the name of the climbing shrub that
had twined itself around the alcove, its pale mauvish

flowers appearing luminous against the evening
light.

She knew that he had answered her, and then went
on to tell her about other different plants that would
soon be flowering, but Corinne's thoughts would not
let her concentrate upon anything else but the
stupendous discovery she had made regarding her
feelings for Juan.

It was then that Juan arrived, and for one long
moment did not say anything but just stood there
grimly surveying them. When he did speak, Corinne
recognised the soft silky voice that she so hated. 'So
here you are,' he said softly, and in those few words
Corinne knew that he was not only angry but absolutely furious. He turned his fury towards Miguel.
'And what was the excuse?' he growled menacingly.
'Room too hot?' he suggested sarcastically.

Miguel jumped up in an action that showed his
nervousness and tried to assume a casual air. 'It was
Diego and Salvador,' he explained hastily. 'Things got
a bit out of hand, so I thought I'd better——'

He did not finish the sentence, he was too concerned about the way that Juan had taken a threaten-
ing step towards him. 'You could have done what the
other guests did, couldn't you?' Juan demanded
harshly. 'They moved into the dining room, but you
couldn't resist the chance, could you?' he added
savagely. 'I'm warning you, Blanco, keep away from
my wife! I won't give you another warning!'

The unwarranted attack on Miguel had taken
Corinne by surprise, but she could not stand by
without making some effort on Miguel's behalf; he
had done nothing to warrant such a virulent display
from Juan. 'I'm sure Señor Blanco didn't——' was as

far as Juan allowed her to get, and his harsh, 'We shall discuss this later,' threat, followed by the haughty command of, 'Come! We are leaving!' left her no choice but to follow Juan's stiff back as he turned and marched back to the house.

Corinne did not see Dolores before they left, although she vaguely thought it would have been more polite of them to say 'thank you' for the party, if nothing else, but Juan's mood was such that even if Dolores had appeared, she very much doubted if such sentiments would have been expressed as she was bundled unceremoniously out of the house and towards Juan's car.

She was still in a state of utter perplexity in regard to Juan's fury at what had only been a kindly thought on Miguel's part, even if it was instigated initially by Dolores.

It was not until the car was sweeping down the drive and out on to the main road that Corinne was presented with quite another picture of the whole episode, and she caught her breath. It was utterly inconceivable, yet it did make some sort of sense, and would certainly explain the reason why Juan had behaved as he had. Her cheeks flamed as she explored this unwelcome explanation, and she was grateful for the darkness of the car's interior.

What sort of a woman did Juan think she was? Did he think she would willingly receive advances from a stranger? Her soft lips firmed. Miguel obviously had a reputation, hence Juan's warning to him to stay away from her, but it took two to have an affair, and Juan had not even given her the benefit of the doubt!

And to think, she mused seethingly, that none of it would have happened if he had returned to her

directly after taking that call, but he had chosen to
linger with his lady love! There was, she told herself furiously, only one reason why neither of them
had heard that crash. Her breath caught on this
thought, and she moved restlessly. What did it matter to her what they were doing? She was only the
whip he was using to bring his woman to heel.

She might be just a tool in his eyes, but she was
still a person in her own right. She had feelings too,
unfortunately for her, a woman's feelings, she
thought bitterly, and wished with all her heart that
Juan had settled for Clair. Clair would have loved
such a situation and would have readily welcomed
the challenge to capture the stony heart of the man
who had married her, in spite of the bald fact that
his heart was firmly entrenched elsewhere.

There was no doubt whatsoever in Corinne's
mind that Clair would have fallen in love with Juan.
She simply did not see how she could have done
otherwise. Men like Juan Martel did not often come
one's way, and were never forgotten by the unlucky
ones whose paths they crossed.

When the car drew up outside the hotel Corinne
knew a profound sense of relief, even though she
knew that Juan had stored up a few choice comments
on her evening's performance, but she only wanted
to get it over with and go to bed. The loud talk and
the unaccustomed attention she had received that
evening from virtual strangers had tired her, and left
her feeling limp and exhausted.

Any hope that Juan might have relented and let
her off the hook was firmly quashed by his harsh,
'Wait for me in your lounge,' as he put her in the

elevator and went off to check that all was well in the hotel section.

When Corinne arrived in the lounge, Joy, wrapped in her dressing gown, and looking very sleepy, appeared at the door that led directly to their rooms. 'Did you have a lovely time?' she asked sleepily.

Corinne was about to answer her when Juan's hard voice cut across the room towards them. 'Go to bed, Joy.'

That was all he said, but there was such heavy authority in his command that Joy's brows lifted slightly as she did as he ordered, casting a quick anxious look towards her sister as she left the room.

'You don't have to take it out on Joy!' Corinne said furiously, as she threw her fur coat on to the nearest chair. She was tired, and at that moment she didn't care if Juan packed the pair of them back to the U.K.! Joy would not like it, but anything was better than this.

Juan surveyed her out of narrowed eyes. 'It's not Joy's behaviour I'm concerned about, it's her sister, my wife,' he said softly but insinuatingly.

'Then in that case, you've nothing to worry about,' Corinne broke in hastily, unable to bear the way that he was lookng at her. 'There was no need for you to have gone for Miguel like that, either,' she tacked on breathlessly, wanting to get that part of it over with in the shortest possible time.

'I think I am a little more qualified to judge his actions than you are,' he replied harshly, 'so you will listen to me and you will do precisely what I tell you to do in the future. You will never, repeat never, be alone in his company again. Is that quite clear? If you happen to find yourself in company and he joins that company, you are to leave immediately.' His lips hardened to a firm line. 'I shall of course make certain that I accompany you on all future gatherings, but there will be times when the unforeseen incident will occur, and that is where this ruling will be enforced. I do not intend,' he said crisply, 'to suffer the indignity of having to search out my wife's whereabouts again—or expect to find her ensconced in private seclusion with such a man as Miguel Blanco. The warning I gave him goes for you too,' he added grimly. 'I shall not repeat it.'

Corinne stood in shocked silence. If she had let Miguel make violent love to her she could not have received a harsher condemnation. He had said he was more qualified to judge Miguel's actions, so he did think the worst of her! The injustice of it all made her retort cuttingly, 'Thank you for being so explicit.' She gave an hysterical chuckle, then commented bitterly, 'I promise to keep my unbridled passions under firm control from now on! Now may I go to bed?' she asked wearily.

Juan gave her a forbidding look and moved over to where she stood, and her eyes met his defiantly but she was poised to head for the door at the first hint of trouble.

'You've got that look in your eye again,' he said softly. 'Remember what I said?' he asked tauntingly.

Corinne's apprehension was echoed in her wide lovely eyes and she took a step backwards away from him. He gave a low chuckle. 'Little fool,' he said softly. 'I'm not about to break our contract—not yet,' he added in a low voice, so low that Corinne wondered if she had heard him say it, or had imagined it. 'Go to bed,' he went on harshly, 'and think about

what happened tonight, and how it must have looked
from an interested onlooker's point of view. Newly
married women do not usually allow themselves to be so
blatantly hoodwinked into what could have turned out
to be a very embarrassing situation. Under the circumstances, I have been very lenient with you. I could
have thrashed you, and there was a time when I very
nearly did.'

He gave a grim nod at the look of utter astonishment on Corinne's face. 'One day you will realise the
truth of this, and that only the fact that you are completely inexperienced and utterly incapable of any such
dealings prevented me from carrying out this punishment.'

Corinne stared at him. A variety of emotions
flowed over her as she acknowledged his blunt
summing-up of the episode. If he had wanted to make
her feel gauche and stupid, then he had succeeded,
she thought numbly. She would far rather have received
the thrashing he had threatened, although she had no
idea just what this entailed, but it would have been
kinder, she thought bitterly, and hated him for his
cruelty.

Her battered senses recalled what he had said about
onlookers, and she gave a twisted smile as she recalled
the way that Dolores Galdós had snatched at the opportunity of seeing him alone. The thought that Juan
had probably engineered the whole thing made her
reply coldly, 'And perhaps you might remember what
happened before I was—' she drew in a deep
breath, finding it difficult to control her words, she
was so furious, 'so—er—hoodwinked. I doubt if
many guests missed seeing Dolores Galdós join you
in that room. Newly married husbands don't usually

encourage such blatant attention from another woman, do they?' she queried sweetly, and got a lot of
satisfaction from the swift darkening of Juan's features. 'Or is there one rule for husbands and another
for wives?' she added, unwisely capitalising on her
triumph. 'Surely, under the circumstances, any wife
might have done precisely the same as I did, just to
get her own back. You didn't exactly rush out to find
out what that crash was about, did you?' she went
on recklessly. 'Your loving wife might have been
under a pile of masonry for all you cared!' she ended
furiously.

Juan's reply was as frightening as it was unex-
pected. He reached out and caught her slim wrist in
a hard savage grip and propelled her towards him so
swiftly that she could do nothing about it, and her
first startled reaction was that she was about to find
out exactly what he had meant by giving her a
thrashing!

When she found herself in a tight hold held against
his lean hard body, and her hands forced behind her
back, she knew that he had quite another purpose in
mind, but still a punishment of a kind. 'My loving
wife,' Juan muttered between clenched teeth, 'had
better watch her words, or she will be exceedingly
bruised in the morning! Who told you about
Dolores?' he asked her harshly, and when Corinne
gave a small negative shake of her head from the
restricted position she was held in, he tightened his
grip on her.

When she still did not reply but made a frantic attempt to break free of him, he imprisoned both her
hands in one of his and brought his other hand up
and placed it under her chin, forcing her to look up

at him. 'Well?' he demanded grimly.

He meant to have an answer and Corinne knew that he would not let her go until she had given him one. She swallowed. She could and did refuse to meet those compelling eyes of his, and gazed steadfastly at his ultra-white shirt collar. She did not want to make trouble for Carmen. 'Miguel,' she replied breathlessly, 'and will you please release me? You've made your point,' she added bitterly.

Juan's grip on her lessened considerably, but he did not release her. 'Miguel,' he repeated in a low voice. 'He didn't waste much time, did he?' he said in a thoughtful way, as if speaking to himself.

His eyes then went slowly over Corinne's features, resting briefly on her soft full lips now slightly parted as she struggled to compose herself. 'The rooms are soundproof,' he said slowly, but significantly. 'If they weren't, you would have been able to hear Dolores' hysterical condemnation of our marriage.'

He continued to stare at her, then slowly let her go. Corinne needed no second bidding and turned towards the door. 'It hurt, did it?' he queried softly.

Corinne paused at this and turned back to face him, her puzzlement at the question plainly visible in her lovely eyes.

'Think about it,' he advised her with a wicked imp of amusement lurking in his eyes.

CHAPTER TEN

CORINNE did think about it, and then wished she hadn't. She might be inexperienced, and not very bright when it came to the perplexities of love, but even she could not fail to see the implications behind those taunting last words of Juan's.

It was even worse to have to acknowledge the truth. It had hurt, but she would never give him the satisfaction of knowing this for certain.

Her eyes narrowed in thought as she put out her bedside light and settled down to sleep. He could have been referring to her pride, of course. He had enough of that ingredient to be able to recognise it in anyone else. It had been pride alone that had made him react so violently to Miguel's protective action.

She gave a deep sigh before sleep overcame her. That had been the first lesson, and no doubt there would be others, but from now on she would do exactly what Juan told her to do. She hadn't particularly liked Miguel Blanco, and his instructions on this would cause her no hardship.

The rest of that week was spent in more sightseeing, although it was plain to see that Joy would rather have been at the salon, and felt that there was plenty of time to take such trips in the future. These thoughts, however, soon dispersed once they were on the tours.

There were many beauty spots on the island, and panoramic views to hold the attention. On one tour to Tejeda they saw a vast crater of volcanic origin, but which was now a deep verdant valley that was farmed by the hardy hill farmers. As Corinne gazed down to the floor of the crater she wondered how, whatever produce was wrested from its depths, it was eventually brought to market, and presumed that it meant a stiff upward climb for the farmers. They would not only have to be fit, she mused, but very strong, and she was about to put this question to Juan when she found him studying her with that enigmatic look in his eye again, and she immediately forgot the question.

It was not the first time that she had found herself under such scrutiny from him, and try as she might, it was not easy to counteract such individual and personal attention from a man of his stamp.

Joy's presence considerably helped to lessen the tension she could feel building up inside her at this totally unfair gambit of his to discomfit her, for she could see no other reason why she had suddenly become the focal point of interest for him.

The following day Juan took them to Agaete by way of a round tour, first visiting Arcus on the northern highway, and following a rather frightening steep incline around the surrounding valleys, they eventually came to a tourist hotel that offered panoramic views for miles around.

As they stood looking out on to the valleys below, Juan pointed out plantations of bananas, for this was the centre of the banana growing industry of the island, and the industry that had been the main source of income for many years. The growing of tomatoes had soon become a secondary source of income, he told them, and now many other products were also exported.

Their next stop was at a banana plantation at Guia, and Corinne and Joy stood gazing at the tightly packed clumps of greenish bananas, smaller than the ones normally seen at home, for there were many species of banana, Juan told them, but the Canarian variety had a distinct flavour of their own and held pride of place on the selling market.

In the valley of Agaete they visited a garden of orange trees, with the ripening fruit hanging invitingly close to their hands, and Corinne, remembering that this was the island's winter period, marvelled at the sight. There were coffee beans growing beside avocado trees, whose fruit, the avocado pear, was of special interest to Corinne who always chose it for a starter if it was on the menu.

That weekend Juan took them to watch the folk dancing in the Pueblo Canario, and as it was Sunday, Carmen joined them. It seemed ages since the girls had seen her, and her company was very welcome.

The dancers were dressed in traditional costume, the girls wearing long skirts beautifully embroidered at the hems and covered by a brightly coloured type of apron, interwoven with lace. A simple white blouse was worn above the skirt, and each wore a small beret with a pom-pom matching the colour of their aprons.

The men wore white pleated skirts that irresistibly reminded one of Grecian dress, with wide black cummerbunds around their waists, and white balloon-sleeved shirts. Their black sombreros were not worn, but held in place by a chin strap and slung over the back of their shoulders. Their brightly coloured boleros vied to match the brightness of their partners' aprons.

Around the dancing area were placed many tables and chairs, so many in fact that only a small square in the middle of the mosaic-tiled courtyard was left for the performers' use. Joy commented on this fact, but was assured by a smiling Carmen that there was ample room for the exhibition.

The dancers had their own accompaniment of musicians, their instruments, which comprised different sized guitars, giving a melodious backing to the slow but utterly charming steps of the dances performed, and the two-hour entertainment passed incredibly swiftly for Corinne and Joy, who had not only enjoyed the dancing but the folk songs sung while the dancers took a well earned rest during the intermission.

After the dancing was finished they wandered through the small shops that displayed items of the island's crafts. Beautifully embroidered blouses and tablecloths were among the numerous goods on sale, and Carmen told them that embroidery was taught at special schools on the island, preserving a craft that had been carried on for centuries, and the young girls were trained to carry on this fine art.

Carmen stayed with them for the rest of that day, and left after dinner that evening, arranging to pick Joy up the following morning for her first day at work.

The thought of Joy's absence until just after four each day depressed Corinne, but she said nothing of this to Joy, not wanting to spoil her eager anticipation at actually earning her living doing the one job she had set her heart on.

How she would cope on her own, Corinne had no idea. It did occur to her that she might wander down to the salon herself, now that she knew where it was —not too often, but it would be somewhere to go. However, on further thought of this possibility, she decided to let well alone. Juan had made a specific point of dissuading her from any such interest, and she would only make trouble for Carmen if she disregarded his wishes. There were the museums, of course, and she supposed she could always fill in some time there, and the cathedral; she had wanted to see the cathedral. She frowned. After these avenues of interest had been exhausted, what other interests could she find to occupy her day?

The following day she waved Joy off, smiling at the excited flurry she had been in to get breakfast over with and not keep Carmen waiting. She did not go down to Reception with Joy, but elected to wave goodbye from the lounge window that looked directly out on to the front of the hotel, and as the car drove off she knew a sense of utter isolation and despondency for the future.

'And what have you in mind for today?' Juan's deep voice asked, cutting across her miserable musings as she watched Carmen's car vanish round the bend of the drive.

Corinne turned to look at him, her wide eyes registering her surprise, for he had never returned this early from the hotel section before, and normally only appeared in time to take lunch with them. 'I hadn't got as far as planning anything,' she replied warily, wondering if he would suggest that she visited one of the museums.

'Good!' he replied brusquely. 'In that case I shall

take you to Maspalomas. It's about time I put in a visit. Are you ready?' he asked, as Corinne just stood there trying to work out why he should take her to Maspalomas. 'You should fetch a head-scarf,' he continued smoothly, 'it can be both windy and hot there.'

As she went to fetch her head-scarf, Corinne wondered what he would have done if she had made any plans for the day. Disregarded them, she thought ironically, for she had a feeling that he had made up his mind to take her with him, and that would be that.

Maspalomas had been one of the places that the girls had not visited, but Juan had said dryly that as it was so near, a visit could be made any weekend, and there were frequent buses laid on for the tourists' use. The resort was on the island's southern shore, and its sandy dunes reminded one of the Sahara, but could be extremely uncomfortable in high winds with the fine golden sand lashing all within its path.

On calmer days the beach was made for sunbathers, and only a few hours of the hot sunshine was needed to produce the evidence of a holiday in the tropics, Juan told Corinne, as he turned off the main highway and took a road leading to a large hotel complex.

Even though they still had a short distance to go before they reached the complex, Corinne could see that it was a private establishment, for the road led only to the hotel and soon they came to an arched entrance over which was hung a signboard that bore the names, 'Mowbray & Martel,' in gold and black lettering.

'They're apartments, actually,' commented Juan, as they swept through the arched entrance and he casually acknowledged the swift salute given him by the uniformed man at the entrance.

Corinne, looking ahead of her, noticed that the complex was built on a hill overlooking the sea, and further down she saw a swimming pool, not a large one, but one that obviously belonged to one of the apartments, and looking a little further to her right, she saw other pools of various designs and patios on which sunbathers were sprawled. This was surely the height of luxury, she thought; not only had the guests private accommodation, but a pool as well, and very probably their own stretch of beach.

The cost of such accommodation would surely be prohibitive, she mused, and she could now understand why Juan had been anxious to gain full ownership of such a lucrative property.

She darted a quick glance at Juan as they drew up beside a large building that was the reception area, and she wondered why he had chosen to bring her there, particularly when she recalled his blunt reply to an early conversation, that his other business dealings were no concern of hers.

When Juan stood beside her outside the door of the building, a sudden thought struck her that he might have relented over the question of a job for her, and her spirits lightened at even the glimpse of a hope in this direction.

They arrived in the plush reception lounge just as a man in a bright red checked shirt and shorts was complaining to the girl behind the desk. His accent proclaimed him to be an American. 'When I said I wanted my bill, I meant today, not tomorrow. I've a connection to make in an hour's time. If you haven't got it ready in fifteen minutes, you'll have to send it on to me,' he declared testily.

Juan's brow darkened as he walked forward towards the desk and the receptionist gave him a visible look of relief. 'Mr Reid's account has been held up,' she said to Juan, and the American turned to face Juan.

'Are you the owner?' he demanded.

Juan gave him a slow nod of confirmation, and before the man could air his grievance he turned back to the pretty blonde receptionist. 'Have you Mr Reid's booking dates?' he asked. At the girl's nod, he turned to the guest who was showing definite signs of increasing impatience. 'I apologise for the inconvenience,' he said quietly. 'We shall charge you only for the accommodation. Make a bill out for Mr Reid, Barbara,' he ordered.

Mr Reid blinked in astonishment, then gave a grin.

'That's mighty handsome of you sir,' he said genially. 'I must say I've no other complaints, everything was first class!' he added appreciatively.

Juan accepted the man's thanks with a brusque nod and looked back at Corinne who had hovered in the background during this discussion, and with a slight incline of his dark head indicated that she was to follow him.

They proceeded through Reception and through a door marked 'Staff. Private' and Corinne found herself in an office full of busy typists and an air of frantic activity.

As Juan strode on ahead of Corinne, he would incline his head now again as he received a welcoming smile from one of the staff, and Corinne felt exactly like an Indian woman as she brought up the rear of

what was turning out to be an almost regal visitation of
the big chief.

They had now arrived at a door marked 'Accounts', and Juan, followed by Corinne, entered the
office.

The office was remarkably quiet after the noisy
clatter of the typists' room, and seemed almost
deserted of staff compared with the other office. Almost as soon as the door had closed behind them, it
was opened again to admit a slight, harassed-looking
man who said in English, 'I've been trying to contact
you. Placido should have been back last Wednesday,
but he's got delayed by the air-controllers' strike.
Even so,' he added apologetically, 'we could have
managed, but it looks like being a long dispute, and
several business men are cutting short their vacations
just in case the disputes spread to other airports. I
understand you dealt with one of them just now,'
he tacked on with a wry grin, then sobered as he
added, 'I'm afraid we shall have to take on some extra
help to cover the crises—er—I know you prefer to
use our own staff, but Rosita is off with an eye infec-
tion, and she's the only one I could use, the others are
only typists and useless at figure work.'

Corinne held her breath and willed herself not to rush
forward with an offer of help. To do so would only
arouse Juan's fury and not help her cause one little bit.
So she just stood by as her mind worked out ways and
means of persuading Juan to let her help out. It was too
good a chance to miss, and she felt that fate was surely
on her side, why else should they have arrived at such an
opportune moment?

Juan gave his reluctant permission for such help
to be recruited, adding authoritatively that he would

personally interview each applicant. He then introduced Corinne to Mr Blake, adding dryly, that here was a compatriot of hers who hailed originally from Devon.

Corinne had known that he was English, for although most of the Islanders that she had met spoke English, their intonations proved that it was not their native language. The thought that the accounts manager was an Englishman seemed to seal her assurance that she would be successful in her quest, and her smile was open and friendly as Juan, telling Mr Blake that he would be in his private suite if he needed to contact him for any other query, ushered Corinne to the door.

As they left the reception building and walked towards a block of apartments, Corinne was in a fever of impatience to get wherever they were going so that she could tackle Juan on the subject.

She scarcely noticed the journey, her mind was too full of the opportunity that had been offered, unwittingly, of course, by the shortage of staff.

Juan's suite was on the ground floor, and Corinne found herself standing in a cool tiled corridor beside a door for which Juan produced a key, and after unlocking it, he stood aside and indicated that she should precede him into the interior.

Her first impression of the large luxurious lounge they entered was completely overshadowed by her urgent need to communicate her wish to Juan, and she hardly noticed the furnishings or the roomy proportions, and was about to speak to Juan when he forestalled her by walking across the room towards a small bureau on which stood a telephone, and calling room service, ordered lunch for two.

Food was the last thing on Corinne's mind, but she was forced to wait until he had made the call.

It seemed an age before he replaced the receiver, and without waiting for any more interruptions she moved towards him quickly, not realising how much urgency she revealed in this small movement and making Juan's eyebrows rise slightly.

'Let me help out in the accounts section, please, Juan,' she pleaded. 'It's the only work I can do.'

Juan's jaw hardened as he looked down at her, and she knew he was going to refuse her request, but she refused to be beaten and laid a pleading hand on his arm. 'Please, Juan,' she whispered coaxingly.

The hope in her eyes quickly faded as she saw his face suddenly close up, and he moved sharply away from her so that her touch was removed from his arm, as if the contact repelled him, she thought bewilderedly, and she moved quickly away in the opposite direction and stood gazing with unseeing eyes out of the window.

A golden sun-drenched beach lay in front of her gaze with a brilliant blue sky above, under which the sun-worshippers lay stretched out in recumbent positions, but Corinne saw none of this. The heat of the tropical sun never reached the arctic regions to where her heart now resided. She could feel the tears gathering at the back of her eyes, but she willed them not to fall.

'I am hoping your time may be better employed,' Juan said softly. 'Come, I will show you over the suite while we wait for luncheon.'

Corinne swallowed. He had left her no room to manoeuvre, and no chance to argue out her case. She followed him out of the lounge with legs that had

lost their springiness. Better employed, she thought
dully, going around museums and taking tea with his
friends' wives. She caught her breath sharply; she
would hate it! If things looked bleak before, they
looked even worse now. He would never change his
mind, and to have been so near to the kind of work
she could do and then to find—she clenched her
hands into small fists.

'This is the dining room,' commented Juan, apparently unaware of the thoughts going through
Corinne's unhappy mind as her bleak eyes swept
around the room they were standing in. It was large
enough to comfortably seat four persons, but Corinne
would not have commented if it had been of banquet-
ing size.

The next room he led her into was a bedroom with
a double bed, and this again barely received a glance
from Corinne, who just wanted the tour over with
and to get back to the hotel where she could work
out what she was going to do about her future. A
future that did not include living at a certain hotel
and playing a role just to suit Juan Martel!

There was another smaller room, that could have
served as a dressing room or a second bedroom but
apparently was used as a makeshift office, judging by
the small desk and files stacked up beside it.

After a brief glimpse into a well-proportioned
bathroom, a shower room and the usual offices, Juan
led her back to the lounge commenting, 'Felipe, my
manager, is in Las Palmas at the moment. You will
eventually make his acquaintance, but I deliberately
chose to call here while he was otherwise occupied.
He's a nice enough fellow, but inclined to be garru-
lous.'

Corinne vaguely wondered why he had bothered to furnish her with this information; the chances were she would never make the manager's acquaintance.

Juan indicated that she should be seated with an elegant wave of his hand towards a comfortable-looking chair beside the window, and when she was seated, settled himself in a chair opposite her. 'He takes his leave at the end of May,' he went on slowly. 'And during that time I take over the management.' His grey eyes met Corinne's disinterested ones. 'This is where we shall stay for a month,' he stated casually, and went on smoothly as if he had been discussing the weather, 'I see no point in travelling back to the hotel each evening, and out again the following morning.'

Corinne's eyes lost their dull expression and widened as the full implication of his words reached her. 'We?' she echoed in a startled voice, as the vision of that double bed rose up like a spectre before her eyes. Then she shook her head in a bewildered movement. She could have not heard correctly, but she had! Her mind searched out for another explanation, and after a moment's thought she had it. This was his manager's apartments, and he must be a married man. She drew in an audible sigh of relief, and gave a slight nod of acknowledgement.

Juan's watchful eyes rested thoughtfully on the now calmer Corinne. 'We,' he repeated, and then gave a small smile. 'I rather thought it would make an ideal honeymoon retreat for us.'

Corinne's eyes registered the shock she had received, and a wicked imp of amusement lingered at the back of Juan's eyes as he witnessed her reaction.

It was this look that gave her the help she so

badly needed at this time. 'I don't think that's at all funny,' she blazed at him, 'not from my point of view anyway,' she added bitterly, and as her fury rose to screaming pitch she tacked on acidly, 'Just because you've taken over a married man's apartment it doesn't mean that you can—' she floundered here, then took a deep breath. 'Well, you know very well what I mean. As far as the rest of the island's concerned, they can think what they like, but I shall expect to find a single bed in that spare bedroom during that month!'

Her hands were trembling when she finished and she clasped them together tightly. She didn't know what she was worried about. May was a long way away, and by then she would be out of this hateful man's vicinity, she told herself in an effort to calm herself. One look at Juan's closed expression, however, told her exactly what she was worried about, and set her pulses racing again.

'A married man's apartment?' Juan echoed with a frown, and his eloquent brows rose. 'This is my apartment. Felipe has a suite over the reception area.' His eyes met Corinne's. 'I have no intention of using the spare room,' he added meaningly. 'I said honeymoon, and I meant honeymoon.' He took in her white face and shocked eyes. 'You just need time to get used to the idea,' he said soothingly.

'You're breaking our contract,' Corinne replied in a voice she hardly recognised as her own; it was all she could think of saying as her mind temporarily closed down on her.

'I apologise about that,' Juan answered, still in that smooth voice as if comforting a child. 'But I did warn you of the possibility. My mind's quite made up. I can assure you we shall deal very well together.'

Unable to bear being in such close proximity to him, Corinne jumped out of her chair and stood beside the window gazing out. There was nothing like having it laid on the line, she thought dully. At least he hadn't tried to fool her that he loved her. At this point she recalled his reaction to the small gesture she had made when she had pleaded with him to give her that job. Her throat constricted painfully. If there was anything worse than marrying a man you didn't love, it was marrying a man who did not love you. Juan loved Dolores, she was certain of this now, he loved her so much that any other woman's touch was abhorrent to him.

She swallowed. 'And you think I would allow——' her voice choked, but she made herself to go on, 'such a thing to happen,' she asked in a low voice. 'Is that the kind of woman you think I am? With no feelings?'

Juan came to stand beside her and caught her hand in his. Corinne tried to pull her hand away, but as before he refused to release it and as he lifted it to his lips, she knew that he was going to kiss her palm, and she also knew what feelings such an action would arouse. 'No!' she said desperately. It was so easy for him, she thought wildly. He could make her his slave and he knew it.

'I know what kind of a woman you are,' Juan said softly, and looked down at her hand trembling in his. 'See how you tremble,' he said gently. 'Like a dove. It trembled once before, remember? It wasn't anger that caused that reaction, was it?' he added softly.

Corinne made another futile effort to release her hand. He was telling her how easy it was going to be for him to lower her defences, and she couldn't bear it. 'And you?' she cried out. 'Will you think of Dolores while you make love to me?'

Her hand was released so suddenly that she had to take a step back from him, and she winced at the look of fury on his face. The next minute he had slapped her across the face, leaving a white mark on her flushed features as she blinked in bewilderment at such an action.

'You will never say that to me again, do you hear?' he said harshly.

'I'm not likely to,' muttered Corinne, still recovering from the blow. Her face stung where he had hit her. 'Do you think we'll deal well together?' she asked him with a twisted smile, as she moved swiftly away from him in an action that said more than words.

'Oh, yes,' he replied grimly. 'When I've tamed that infuriating streak of yours to annoy me. You see now how easily you can goad me into losing my temper. No other woman has that distinction. Is that what you want to hear?' he asked savagely. 'Not even Dolores reached through that far.'

Corinne sat down on the chair again. Because they annoyed each other it didn't mean that they were meant for each other, she thought dully. It usually meant the opposite, but it was no use telling him that, not when he was trying to convince himself that he was in love with her. That, she reasoned silently, was the reason why he had hit her just now. He couldn't bear the truth.

There was a tap on the door, and at Juan's authoritative *'Entrar!'* a waiter appeared wheeling a trolley which he took through to the dining room. A few minutes later he announced that lunch was ready, and stood by the dining room door ready to serve them their meal, but at Juan's sharp command of dismissal he looked surprised, but obeyed the order and left them.

Juan looked at Corinne, and she met his look with a defiant challenge in her dark blue eyes. 'I shall have to do something about that look too,' he said grimly. 'Come and have lunch. I ordered it especially for you. Afterwards we'll talk.'

Corinne wanted to say that food would choke her. She had never felt less like eating, but it was safer to just do as he asked, she thought. That way she might get out of the apartment in one piece.

As she passed him as he stood by the dining room door, it occurred to her that she was not afraid of him, and surely she ought to have been. This puzzled her a little, and she wondered if she was now shock-proof, and considering what she had been through since she had met this domineering man this was not altogether surprising.

When he had seated her at the dining table, in much the same way as a head waiter might have seated a valued client, he sat opposite her and proceeded to tempt her with the dishes of various foods laid out in appetising array.

If he could act as if nothing had happened, so could she, she told herself stoutly, and attempted to try and raise some appetite. Normally, she was very fond of the large succulent prawns that were almost a meal in themselves, but she shook her head as Juan presented a bowl of them to her. He next presented a dish of a creamy-looking substance, murmuring, 'It's mainly cheese, but with a cream base—try it on one of these slivers of toast. It's a great favourite with our European tourists,' he assured her.

If only to look as if she was trying, Corinne smeared a little of the substance on the thin finger of toast and gingerly tasted it. It was creamy, and had an odd cheesy taste, but it was not a cheese that she could identify.

As if in answer to her unspoken query Juan said, 'It's cheese made from goats' milk. The islanders have made cheese this way for centuries.'

Corinne nodded abstractedly, and finished eating the slice of toast, but refused a second piece, saying hastily, 'It was very nice, but I think I'll just have a peach now. I'm not really hungry,' she added, thinking what an absurd situation she was in.

She had just been informed by the forbidding-looking man sitting opposite her that she was to become his bride within a matter of weeks, and here they were sitting at the food table as if nothing untoward had happened, as if this sort of thing was commonplace. Her bemused eyes watched as Juan picked up the fruit bowl and held it towards her with the same studious care that he had offered her the other food, and she was reminded of another custom that also went back centuries, when the native girls were fattened up for their marriages in the belief that they would bear their husbands sturdy sons. A surge of hysteria bubbled up on the thought that perhaps Juan—she swallowed hastily, and in an effort to control these wayward thoughts she attacked the peach as if it were enemy number one, and scraped the silky skin off with more fervour than was necessary.

This apparently offended Juan's sensibilities, and he gave a slight shudder and with a, 'No, no, *mi querida,*' he removed the peach from her grasp, and selecting another one, he then pared it carefully and cut it in thin slices for her.

As Corinne suffered the indignity of having her food cut up for her, she wondered what the word '*querida*' meant, but decided not to seek enlightenment. He was probably calling her stupid, in which case, she would rather not know.

The coffee tray had been left on the dining room sideboard, and when Corinne had finished the peach and said that she was replete, Juan carried the tray into the lounge saying that they would be more comfortable there.

Now that the cease-fire period was over, Corinne knew that she would have to have her wits about her if she was to succeed in her quest to extricate herself from Juan's determined plan for her future.

After handing her her coffee and collecting his, Juan walked over to the chair opposite hers and sat down with an air of deceptive casualness. 'We shall talk about the future, and about the past,' he said quietly. 'As Dolores is in the past, we shall begin there,' he stated firmly.

Corinne put her coffee cup down hastily on the small casual table beside her. 'No, really,' she protested quickly, feeling a flush stain her cheeks. 'It's nothing to do with me—and I apologise for what I said——' she broke off lamely, not knowing how far it was safe to go in that direction.

'It is everything to do with you,' Juan replied inexorably. 'I will not have whispers and rumours ruining our marriage. Dolores,' he went on before Corinne could utter another protest at the autocratic way that he had presumed that she would not oppose his wish to break their contract and make the marriage a real one, 'ceased to exist in my affections,' he gave an ironical smile at this, 'if she ever did hold them,' he added musingly, and gave Corinne a direct stare. 'Perhaps I'd better go back even further. We grew up together, our parents were close friends,' he studied his long tapered hands. 'In those days she was a small, shy, and lovely girl, and I assumed the position of protector towards her. There was never a plan that we should marry. I think perhaps the fact that we had grown up together made us appear more like brother and sister in our parents' eyes than husband and wife, and for that I am eternally grateful,' he added fervently. 'When she was seventeen, a husband was found for her,' he continued steadily. 'A man very much older than she was.' He gave a shrug of his broad shoulders. 'It was then that I mistook sympathy for love—I didn't know it at the time, though,' his fine grey eyes pierced Corinne's dark blue ones, 'and I might never have known it,' he added significantly. 'For Dolores' sake I tried to persuade her parents from forcing her into such a marriage, but I was unsuccessful, of course. Spanish marriage contracts are not easily broken, and this one entailed a great deal of property.'

He gave Corinne a small smile. 'You are more fortunate than Dolores was. Her courtship period was limited to the minimum time allowed. A wise move on the parents' behalf, she was given no time to back out of the arrangement.'

It struck Corinne that there was little difference in Dolores' situation and hers, in spite of what Juan had said, for she was to be given no time to back out

of the consummation of the marriage Juan was insisting on either!

'So,' he continued, 'Dolores married Carlos, who
was wealthy and gave her all that she asked for. Had
it not been for the differences in their ages I believe
she would have been well satisfied with her lot. The
age gap, however, proved the stumbling block. Carlos'
friends were that much older than Dolores', and she
was starved of company of her own age. Carlos,
though kind in many ways, was extremely jealous of
Dolores' friends, particularly the male ones.' His
glance rested on Corinne. 'I can now sympathise
with him,' he said softly. 'I know exactly how he
felt.'

Corinne looked away quickly from the possessive
look in his eyes.

'As a childhood friend of Dolores' I was the only
one he trusted. As a result, I saw more of her than
any of her other friends. I also,' he added a little
grimly, 'became her confidante in times of stress.
She came to depend upon me for company, and to
save her, as she put it, from growing old before her
time.'

He finished his coffee swiftly and held out his
hand for Corinne's cup. 'More coffee?' he queried,
and at the shake of her head, he gave an ironical
smile. 'You want to get it over with, don't you?' he
asked her. 'Well, you must bear with me. I intend
that you shall hear the whole of it.'

Corinne's gaze followed his tall frame as he walked
over to the table to replenish his cup. Just how far
did this sympathy act go? she wondered. If he
thought that he was in love with Dolores there would
have been plenty of chances of—she felt a stab at her

heart; she didn't want to know about that.

'I can assure you that I did at no time betray the trust Carlos had placed in me,' he said softly, as he walked back to his chair, and Corinne gave a start at his astute guess at her thoughts.

'The years went by and I became convinced that I loved Dolores, and certain that at some time in the future she would become my wife. I never questioned this assumption.' He gave an ironical smile. 'There's an old saying that one should be wary of what one wishes for, because it might be granted.' He looked down at the blue and gold coffee cup in his hand. 'And that is precisely what happened to me,' he looked up suddenly at Corinne, catching her unawares. 'Or would have done had I not been privileged to learn the difference between love and sympathy.'

His lean forefinger traced the golden rim of the cup with a caressing movement, and watching, Corinne felt a soft glow inside her, as if it was her cheek he was caressing and not the lip of the cup.

'I am not usually given to outbursts of fury,' he said quietly. 'I always abhorred such exhibitions, and felt that such emotions as jealousy were confined to the vagaries of youth. It never occurred to me to be jealous of Dolores' new-found friends, of which there were a generous sprinkling of men, but even this strange situation did not enlighten me.' His eyes swept lingeringly over Corinne's slight figure. 'It took a slight, brown-haired girl, with enormous dark blue eyes, and with an infuriating habit of speaking her mind, not only with that soft voice of hers, but with those lovely eyes, to pitch me out of my complacency. I wanted to strangle Miguel that night,' he went on steadily. 'Even though I knew he would not dare overstep the bounds of propriety with you, but it made no difference to my feelings. Feelings,' he added meaningly, 'that I had never experienced before, that I did not know that I possessed. I was furious with you too, for stealing my heart in that underhand way. It was only too obvious that you cared nothing for me, and why should you? I had not exactly paved the way for better relations between us, had I, but used you as a foil against Dolores' increasing possessiveness that was becoming a bore.'

'I feel sorry for Dolores,' Corinne broke in, unable to contain her feelings.

Juan got up and stood beside her and looked down at her. 'No, *mi querida*,' he said softly. 'You would have been right to feel sorry for her if I had married her—for me too, come to that, for it would have been a most unhappy liaison. You see, I have a lot in common with her late husband, Carlos, even though I have not yet reached his advanced years. She would have found herself as fettered as before, not for reasons of jealousy, but for reasons of pride. One day I will thank Miguel for not only hastening an event that was sure to take place some time in the future, but for giving me hope that one day you might learn to care for me.'

Corinne recalled the scene that night when Juan had caught her in his arms, holding her in that tight hard hold against him, and her heart thudded at the recollection. She also remembered his last words to her after he had asked her if she was jealous of Dolores.

Her eyes went slowly over Juan's hard handsome features, and moved to his arms that were now held down at his sides. His eyes spoke of his love for her, but his stance suggested a holding back, and she was inevitably reminded of the way that he had moved away from her touch earlier. She knew a feeling of utter desolation. By his own admission he had convinced himself that he loved Dolores. How much easier would it have been for him to convince himself that he loved her. More convenient too, she thought miserably.

Her lovely eyes spoke her doubts, and Juan said softly, 'I could convince you——' his firm mouth hardened. 'Or I could badly frighten you.' He held out his hands before him and stared at them. 'They are not quite steady,' he said quietly. 'I want to hold you in my arms, to crush you to me, to kiss those soft lips of yours and prevent you from objecting. You came very close to such treatment when you pleaded with me to give you that job,' he said harshly. 'The way you looked at me, and the way you said my name.'

He turned abruptly away from her and walked over to the window and stood gazing out. 'I ask leave to court you,' he said. 'I know I'm not giving you much time, but eight weeks should be long enough to convince you of my sincerity. I warn you I do not intend to fail.'

Corinne looked at his tall proud figure, and her heart filled with love for him. She could guess how much it had cost him to put a rein on his feelings for her, for that was not his way. In this alone had he shown her that he truly cared for her. In the days to come she was to wonder how she had captured the heart of such a man, but all she wanted now was to feel his arms about her, and the feel of those firm lips of his on hers.

She got up and walked over to him. 'Could we start now?' she asked him in a deceptively timid voice. 'Our courtship, I mean.'

Juan swung round and his eyes searched her limpid ones, then with a sudden gasp of understanding he caught her to him, his lips finding hers with swift accuracy, and she heard him say one word before his lips descended upon hers.

'What does *querida* mean?' she asked him shyly, a little later on.

'It means *beloved*,' whispered Juan against her lips. 'You will always be my *querida*,' he added huskily, as he drew her back into his arms again.

Choose from this great selection of early Harlequins—books that let you escape to the wonderful world of romance!*

*Some of these book were originally published under different titles.

Relive a great love story...
with Harlequin Romances
Complete and mail this coupon today!

Harlequin Reader Service

In U.S.A.
MPO Box 707
Niagara Falls, N.Y. 14302

In Canada
649 Ontario St.
Stratford, Ontario, N5A 6W2

Please send me the following Harlequin Romance novels. I am enclosing my check or money order for $1.25 for each novel ordered, plus 59¢ to cover postage and handling.

☐ 422	☐ 509	☐ 636	☐ 729	☐ 810	☐ 902
☐ 434	☐ 517	☐ 673	☐ 737	☐ 815	☐ 903
☐ 459	☐ 535	☐ 683	☐ 746	☐ 838	☐ 909
☐ 481	☐ 559	☐ 684	☐ 748	☐ 872	☐ 920
☐ 492	☐ 583	☐ 713	☐ 798	☐ 878	☐ 927
☐ 508	☐ 634	☐ 714	☐ 799	☐ 888	☐ 941

Number of novels checked @ $1.25 each = $_____

N.Y. and Ariz. residents add appropriate sales tax. $_____

Postage and handling $_____ .59

TOTAL $_____

I enclose _____
(Please send check or money order. We cannot be responsible for cash sent through the mail.)

Prices subject to change without notice.

NAME _____
(Please Print)

ADDRESS _____

CITY _____

STATE/PROV. _____

ZIP/POSTAL CODE _____

Offer expires June 1, 1981.

01256337141